Falling for the Beast

Skye Warren

Chapter One

Blake

Three weeks until the end of semester

BLAKE MORRIS STARED down at his coffee, trying to force his sluggish mind to wake up. His throat was dry. His whole body ached, as if reminding him of what he had lost, of the emotional IED that had gone off when he and Erin had gone on a break.

Two weeks of not touching her, not smelling her.

Not feeling her sweet body surrender underneath him.

He saw her in class, but that only made the pain more acute. She was forever in front of him, apart from him—and he, in a constant state of wanting.

The sound of tires on gravel drew his attention to the window. A beat up sedan pulled to a stop in his driveway. His heart began to thud with a hope he could not afford. She was no longer his.

If she'd come to fight for him, he would have to turn her away. And if she'd come to curse him out, it was no better than he deserved.

If it were only his reputation at stake, he would throw it away in a second. It was hers. The woman always took the blame in this situation. He wouldn't let that follow her around, even if it killed him.

He felt like shit for fucking her.

He felt like shit for *not* fucking her.

It was one hell of a conundrum, but the only thing he knew for sure was that he couldn't wait to see her. The brief moments in class were not nearly enough.

He was starved for the sight of her.

The doorbell didn't ring. Knuckles didn't knock. She still had a key, and he supposed she was using it. Footsteps came from behind him. He turned slightly.

Ah, there she was.

Hopeful. Bright. There wasn't any accusation in her brown eyes, so he supposed she had come to fight for him. Somehow that made it worse. He wasn't one hundred percent sure he would win this fight, not when he wanted so badly to lose.

She sat down on the stool next to his. They were seated at the granite bar that capped his kitchen, the same place where they'd shared a light breakfast so many mornings. He made her pancakes once. "Hey, stranger."

There were things he should say to her. *You shouldn't be here.* That much was true. *I don't want you here.* That would be a lie, though it almost definitely would make her leave. He couldn't say the words through the lump in his throat.

Hey, stranger, she'd said.

So he would play along with her game, for now. That seemed to be the only thing he was capable of doing. If only she were a little bit less pretty, a little bit less strong. If he loved her just one fraction less. "Do I know you from somewhere?" he said, his voice rough.

"We may have met. I think you taught one of my college courses."

If the course were really in the past, if it were over, then he could touch her, kiss her. He wouldn't be her professor in the future. It was only the present that hurt so much. "So tell me, how'd I do?"

"Oh, excellent. You got five chili peppers on the professor rating site." At his raised eyebrow, she explained, "That means you're hot."

He swallowed the remainder of his coffee.

"Now I know you're lying."

"I would rate you six chili peppers if I could."

Even though she was just being kind, something panged in his chest. She meant he was beautiful on the inside, or she'd just gotten used to the way he looked, and it was more than enough for him. "Why did you come?" he asked softly.

She glanced down at her clothes, which he now realized where the same stretchy material she wore when she cleaned his house. "I'm here to work."

His eyebrow raised. "You are?"

"You fired me because we were sleeping together. We're not doing that anymore, so there's no reason why I can't vacuum and dust and do the dishes."

A throb in his chest. "Erin—"

"Don't tell me it's a conflict of interest for a student to work for her professor. People do it all the time as research assistants or teaching assistants."

God, the temptation to say yes overpowered him. It was impossible to say no. And it was equally impossible to say yes. He wanted Erin a thousand ways. Over him. Under him. He even longed to take her out in public, on lunches and trips to the museum and evenings at the Tangle-wood symphony. And once the semester was over, he would do all those things.

If she would still have him.

"I can't let you clean for me," he said, his voice thick with regret.

Her brown eyes turn glossy with unshed tears. "Is it just that you don't want me anymore? I wish you'd just say so. It would hurt, but at least then I'd know—"

"God, Erin, no. I never should have let you pick up a broom around here. Even then, before I had ever touched you, when I believed I never would, I knew it was wrong. I want to serve you. It should never be the other way around."

She slipped off the stool and circled him. He couldn't keep his eyes off her legs. Her slender legs cupped by the soft fabric of her leggings. Her fingertips brushed over his shoulders. "I want to see you, Blake. That's all. If I have to clean your house that's a small price to pay."

Her lush breasts pressed against his back. He shut his eyes, holding back his groan. His thickening erection tented his sweatpants. "You wouldn't clean my house."

Her breath coasted over the back of his neck. "I would."

Tugging her wrist, he pulled her around to stand between his knees. "I wouldn't let you, not when I could touch you. Not when I could taste you."

Her lashes dropped low. "Don't make me leave. Not yet."

No. Now that he had seen her he would have to have her. Which was proof that she could never come back here. His willpower wasn't strong enough. A brick wall fortified with steel and carbonite wouldn't be strong enough. Nothing could combat the sweet sensuality she exuded.

She knelt in front of him and every thought, every teasing quip flew out of his brain. He could see the shadow between her breasts through the low V of the tank top she wore. Her eyes were heavy lidded with arousal. She tugged the band of his sweatpants down, releasing his heavy, full cock into her palm. She held him up, as if testing his weight. Her palm looked small and pale beneath the ruddy girth of him.

Delicate fingers wrapping around pulsing, hungry flesh.

"*Erin.*"

"I know," she whispered. "It hurts, doesn't it?"

Jesus. Every time they were together she grew

surer in her feminine power, and every time he fell further in love with her. The bonds gripped him tightly, but he never fought them. Here, with Erin, was exactly where he wanted to be.

He sucked in a breath. "Oh, baby, *yes*, like that. Harder."

"Don't make me leave," she whispered again, brushing her lips to the crown of his cock.

He pushed the hair back from her face, enjoying the silvery play of sunlight on the crown of her head. Her position was sensual, but when he looked down at her, the emotions he felt far surpassed the physical. Her position was submissive, but he was the one at her mercy.

With a wicked tilt of her lips, she fisted his cock and brought him to the brink, pump after groan-inducing pump. Just when he was sure he'd blow, she stopped, leaving him on the knife-thin edge of pleasure and aching need. Her hand remained still, holding him up as she leaned forward.

Her lips pressed the slippery head in a chaste kiss. The velvety caress made his hips cant forward. He sighed in helpless denial. She was killing him, slaying him, and he wouldn't have stopped her for anything. Her tongue darted out, sending molten pleasure to his balls. She sucked him in shallowly, holding the head in her mouth and sucking hard. He swore every crude, vulgar word he'd ever heard in the military, his fingers white-knuckled on the edge of the stool.

She glanced up at him. The sultry knowledge in her eyes mesmerized him. His veined shaft disappeared between her stretched, pink lips. He wanted so many things. To make her take him deeper. To hold her head. To own her. But his love for her wrapped around him like butter-soft chains, holding him back and keeping her safe.

A new, subtle pressure had him clenching and rising up to meet her mouth. She'd worked a finger down below where he couldn't see—but Jesus, he could feel. Sparks down the seam of his balls and up underneath. How could she bear to touch him there? He wanted to make her stop, to force her to rub him there faster and harder. The barstool may as well have been glued to his palms. He couldn't move them. Couldn't stop her, couldn't make her do a damn thing. This was all her: wicked intent and lavish attention.

Slowly, her finger slid back farther, to the waiting pucker of his ass. His whole body strung up tight. He clenched his jaw to keep from crying out *no* and *stop* and *God fuck yes*. Flames licked his balls, and he rocked in a rhythmic motion, desperate for relief.

As her finger explored forbidden territory, her eyes held a question. *Do you like this?* And they held something else, her answer. She liked this, and he was filled with gratitude. Flushed with pleasure. He would probably go up in smoke any second now, but God, the burn felt so sweet.

Circles.

The thought pierced his lustful haze. She was making circles right there with the tip of her finger. He followed the sensation of tiny spirals at his most vulnerable point. She sucked him in deep, making his eyes roll back. Her grip at the base of his cock tightened and then slid along the shaft. Her finger at his back entrance pressed inside. The smallest degree of entry, and he was lost. Climax swept over and consumed him. He shouted something broken and base while he poured his orgasm on her tongue. Shudders wracked his body as he stared down at her. His entire body clenched tight with pleasure before relaxing in sweet contentment. She lovingly licked the last traces of seed from his cock.

Finally releasing himself, he unclenched his fingers from the stool. One hand shoved into her hair and gently pulled her to him. He kissed her with an open mouth and greedy tongue, tasting himself inside her. His body was sated, but not his desires. He had wanted to taste her, and judging from the way she shivered in his grip, she wanted that too.

Feeling wild and desperate, he glanced around the kitchen. Through the open-air entranceway, he saw the armchair in the living room. Not a very comfortable piece, but the padding would protect her. He wanted to make her come so hard her liquid spilled onto the cushion. He felt feral, wanting to mark the furniture with her scent, her sex.

"Follow me." Feeling grim and unkind, he pulled her over and sat her down. A little more roughly than he needed to, but it set the tone. She needed to understand. This was how it would be, him leading and her placid. It was the only way he could worship her properly, because if she spoke a single word, he'd obey.

He spread her legs, placing them over each padded arm of the chair. It was bondage without a foot of rope. The more he pleasured her, the tighter her legs would bind her here. Of course, she could always relax and stand up herself, but she wouldn't. The dark amusement in her eyes said she understood the game, she accepted it. Her parted lips and quickened breath said she didn't give a damn, as long as he gave her what she needed.

The folds of her sex glistened in the faint light. He speared his fingers through the moisture, relishing the slickness. So lovely. And his, all his. He dipped into the wet heat. His cock stirred again, ready to take its rightful place. No. Not this time. He quested farther north, to the place where softness bundled together, where gentle pleasure tightened into nerves. He stroked her clit, and she shuddered.

"Blake."

She sounded lost and beautiful. What was he doing to her? Should he stop? Leave her alone? He couldn't.

"Stay quiet," he said. "Keep your hands on the chair. If you speak or move, I'll stop."

He leaned forward to breathe in the earthy, sweet scent of her. Fuck, he went crazy for this. The first taste had him rock hard. The second made him groan with fevered longing. Her sex was plump and swollen, slippery against his lips. He found the well of arousal with his tongue, drawing out more liquid and drinking it down.

The familiar musk of her transported him to another world, where time could never intrude. He had an eternity to lap her folds and suckle her clit. He lashed her with his tongue, pulling stuttered breaths and harsh inhalations, but she was so good. So obedient. She remained almost silent, almost still.

He glanced up and lost a heartbeat at what he saw. Her unfocused eyes had glazed with unshed tears. Her parted lips trembled. He had meant to draw this out, to make her wait and maybe return the favor by exploring the tight pucker beneath. But he couldn't stand to see her in this kind of sexual agony.

Pressing two fingers inside, he found the roughened spot that made her buck. His lips closed around her clit, sucking her hard. Her whole body grew taut. Her hips bucked against his face. The sensual violence grew too hard, too much, until he skated his free hand, still damp from her juices, along the tender insides of her thighs, a feathery caress to push her over.

She cried out her release as wetness flowed over his lips and down his chin, coating the chair just like he'd imagined. He helped her back down with slight licks and soft kisses. When her body slumped against the back of the chair, he picked her up and held her until the trembling subsided.

Her breathing evened out, and for a minute he thought she'd fallen asleep. Her voice sounded drugged when she spoke, slurred and breathy. "Don't make me leave."

A sharp pain lanced his chest. "Not yet."

He kissed the top of her head and let his lips linger there, reveling in the silky strands of her hair. His one, his only. His everything. And he needed to send her away.

ERIN

ERIN RODRIGUEZ SAT at the granite bar top and took a sip of the coffee that Blake had poured for her. He had also added the right amount of cream and sugar. He knew what she liked.

Blake sat down in the chair where she'd just been. He was naked, one ankle slung over the other. Strong hands that could be impossibly gentle hung loosely on either side of the chair. He leaned his head back against the chair, eyes closed.

His expression was so peaceful, she couldn't help but stare. Her face flushed when she realized he must feel proof of her excitement beneath him. She might have been more embarrassed except she was distracted by his next words.

"You really do have to go, Erin."

Her heart clenched. "Why are you doing this?"

He leaned forward, looking grim and one-hundred percent serious. "Look, I did handle Melinda. That's done. But someone like her can come back and ruin this, ruin *you*, because of what we're doing. I can't risk your future that way."

"What if I want to take that risk?"

"I'm saying no." His voice was soft, rich with grief but no regret. "I've taken advantage of you for too long already. I never should have touched you. I knew that from the start."

"You're not taking advantage of me." She felt shocked, hollowed out. And somewhat offended. As if she were a child incapable of making her own choices.

He grimaced, seeming to read her thoughts. "You have every right to be mad, but I hope you'll try to understand. My obligation to you goes beyond that of a lover. I'm your professor. I have a responsibility to take care of you."

She was silent, hating that she did understand. She loved his integrity, and that's what she was seeing now. How could she fault him for what made him Blake?

"I hated facing this decision," he said. "Either way, I would lose you."

Her stomach bottomed out. "Why does it

have to be forever? I'm graduating in a few weeks. The summer session will be over. We can be together freely."

"I don't want you to commit to anything."

"God, Blake. You don't want me to commit? As if I haven't already committed in every possible way with my body? With my heart? I'm already committed."

His resolve seemed to crack. "Erin…"

"Please, Blake."

"The day after the Faculty Ball."

"The Faculty Ball?"

"It marks the end of the semester. By then class will be over, grades will be submitted, and your thesis will be finished. If you still want me then, I'm yours."

Her heart swelled. She loved him. And forever… well, she would do just about anything for forever with him. Even give him up for a while.

"Okay," she said, still feeling unsteady. "I'll agree to that, if you agree to my terms."

"Which are?"

"We wait until after the Faculty Ball, and then you come home with me."

"I've been to your apartment before."

"I meant my hometown. Come home and meet my mother. It will be better than having her meet you here, where she'll…" Swallowing, she looked around his kitchen. The thick crown molding and stainless-steel appliances. "Well, she *might* judge you based on your house."

Standing, he stalked toward her. God, completely naked. Why couldn't she stop staring?

Reaching behind her neck, he pulled her in and kissed her flush on the nose. "Did you just invite me to meet the parents?" he teased. "This must be serious."

She nodded. "Well, there's only one parent. But yes, I'd say it's serious."

"Glad to hear it, because I'm serious too. And I might have terms of my own."

"Which are?"

"I want you to move in with me. Not as the maid or as my student. As my lover."

Her breath hitched. She glanced around the stately home. "Here?"

"That was the idea. Unless you don't like it."

"No, it's not that. I love your house." Something held her back from saying yes. Being under his control, financially, physically. She'd struggled and studied and worked her whole life so she'd never have to answer to a man. Even though she knew he'd never hurt her, it was hard to give up that dream. "I just meant…I spend all my time here anyway."

His expression was soft and painfully under-standing. "It would be different if you were with me, every day. Every night. But it's okay. You don't have to answer now. After the semester. It can wait."

Her sigh held relief and gratitude. "Thank you."

"I won't rush you, because I need you to be sure. Once you're with me, I'm not going to be able to let you go."

She shivered at the dark note of possession in his voice. After her exams, she'd be able to think straight. Then she'd tell him yes, wouldn't she? She couldn't imagine telling him no. Her love for him posed a greater threat than a domineering man ever could. Blake had gotten under her skin and buried deep in her soul. There would be no going back from this. She was looking over a ledge she knew she would jump over, gauging the distance. If she were honest, she was already on her way down.

"Just promise me something," he said. "I may not always be near you, but I will never be far away. If you're ever in trouble or need something, you let me know. Promise me."

She melted, her heart a puddle. "Oh, Blake."

He gave her a crooked smile. "Nothing is too small. You need a light bulb changed or find a spider in the shower, I'm there."

"Okay, okay," she said with mock forbearance, even though she found it sweet as hell.

Her old boyfriend, Doug, had only been interested in her when they were together. And her mother, as wonderful as she was, had enough to manage with her work that she didn't concern herself with how Erin did on a day-to-day basis.

Especially lately, when she couldn't even seem to take a phone call.

Just as quickly, he turned the topic to safer ground. "So, it's been a long time since I met any parents. I'm not even sure what that entails."

She grinned. "Better mind your manners."

He put a hand to his chest. "I'll be on my best behavior. She isn't going to put us in separate rooms, is she?"

"I doubt it, considering there's just the one bedroom beside hers. Though I suppose we could always make you sleep on the couch."

"Can't blame her. I have the worst intentions where you are concerned." He grew serious. "It can wait until after the summer semester, right?"

"Yes, of course. The drive is too long to make in a weekend trip anyway. We'll spend a few days there. Plus, if you don't mind, we should take your car. I don't think mine has that many miles left in it."

"I don't like you driving that thing."

She rolled her eyes. "It's fine."

He frowned.

She turned away to hide her smile, secretly pleased at his protectiveness. In a minute, he was right behind her, bending her over the barstool.

"Did you just roll your eyes at me, young lady?"

"What are you going to about it?" she taunted him.

"Something wicked. That's what you were hoping for, wasn't it?"

Yes. But she protested feebly, "We just did that."

He pressed down on the small of her back. His fingers played along the inside of her thighs, roaming higher. "If I'm going to be without you for three weeks, I'll need something to tide me over. So let's see. At least once a day, usually. And I won't see you for...far too many days. Think we can make it all up now?"

She huffed a laugh, but her eyes widened when he didn't laugh too. He couldn't be serious.

"I agree," he said conversationally. "That

many times in a single day seems excessive. Five ought to do it."

Even five times was a lot…she'd get chafed. Wouldn't she? Unless she was very, very wet. "You wouldn't really."

He bent to her ear, whispering, "Watch me."

Chapter Two

Erin

Two weeks until the end of semester

TEARS STREAMED DOWN Erin's face by the time Cary Grant kissed Deborah Kerr in monochrome, finally discovering why she hadn't met him that fateful night at the Empire State Building.

"If anything had to happen to either of us...why did it have to be *you*?" Cary Grant said in heartbreaking tenor on the television. She watched the emotional exchange in unabashed tears.

Late night TV sans cable didn't leave many options, but when she'd seen *An Affair to Remember* in the listings, it had resonated with her. The lovers had been apart for six months, whereas she hadn't seen Blake in seven days. So, okay, maybe she was being overly dramatic. But even though they'd seen each other on the sly over the semester, she longed for a time when their relationship could be public.

And permanent.

"If you can paint...I can walk. The world can turn upside down...if..."

The music played, and Erin used another tissue to blow her nose. God. What a movie. *The world can turn upside down.* Yes, she knew something about that. Everyone did, if they'd ever been in love. It turned the world upside down and sideways—and only Blake looked right to her. Only he stood beside her.

She couldn't continue down this line of thought. It would make her too sad, and she was already weepy from the movie. She surveyed her snack food leftovers with dismay. A big mess. She could clean other people's houses, no problem, but her tiny apartment always seemed to fill up with junk. With a press of the remote, the TV flicked off, plunging the room into darkness. Problem solved.

Scratching from the door told her someone was here. She'd never given Blake a key, but her heart still fluttered as if it might be him. In the dark, she rolled her eyes at herself. She had it bad for him.

Courtney slipped inside the apartment and locked the door. She had crept halfway to her bedroom when Erin spoke.

"Had a good night?"

Courtney squeaked. "I thought you'd be asleep."

"Couldn't sleep. I was just watching a movie."

"Oh, well." Courtney stood there awkwardly.

Erin narrowed her eyes suspiciously. What the hell had gotten into her roommate? Her stance looked faintly guilty, like a teenager caught out for the night, even though neither girl had kept tabs on the other. Wait a second...

"You got back together with Derek, didn't you?"

With an embarrassed sound, Courtney flopped onto the couch beside her. "Yes. Okay. Is that so bad?"

"Yes," Erin replied. "No, that's not what I meant. I mean, you can do what you want. No one can judge you for your choices, least of all me."

"But you don't approve."

Well... no, she didn't. Derek was a bit of a douchebag. He didn't appreciate Courtney; he just called her when he was bored. "I just think you can do better, that's all. You're gorgeous, you're smart."

"He's a good catch," she said defensively.

"I know," Erin agreed, knowing there was no way to win this fight. If she trashed Derek, she'd push her friend away.

With a flurry of plastic wrappers, Courtney dug around in the mess on the coffee table until she found the popcorn. "I know how he comes off. And maybe I could do better, but..."

"But?"

"But not everyone can find someone who's perfect. A soldier, a professor. He's kind to you, he's crazy about you. You basically hit the boyfriend jackpot."

A slow smile spread across her face. "Yeah. I did, didn't I?" Abruptly her smile faded. "Oh man, now I really want to see him."

"Girl, you have it bad."

Erin groaned, turning her face into the lumpy throw pillow. "I know."

"How's your thesis going?"

"Okay. I had the interview today." She didn't need to explain which interview. All of the interviews she'd done for her thesis were emotional and important. Only one was personal. The intern had reluctantly agreed to talk to her on the phone.

"So the senator's guilty?"

"I'm not sure. She said it was all a misunderstanding."

"Oh shit. That means he's guilty *and* he paid her off."

"Or he threatened her," I muttered, glum in the face of these options.

"So are you going to tell the jackpot?"

"And make him choose between me and his family? No, thank you. I've been down this road before. It ends with me stranded with no car."

CHAPTER THREE

BLAKE

One week until the end of semester

BLAKE STRETCHED AND blinked watery eyes at his laptop screen, blinding in the dark room. In the days since he and Erin had cut contact, he had written twenty pages of a grant. The kind of grant he would write if he were to join the university as a full-time faculty member. He thought it was pretty good too. He was excited to share it with Erin. That would have to wait until the semester was over and he could see her again.

Fuck, he missed her. Already his concerns about their relationship had dwindled low, but this separation had squashed any lingering doubts.

Once, he had needed her. He'd leaned on her strength and followed her light. Now, he knew that he could live without her. It was dry and boring and cold, but he could do it. He just didn't want to. His desire for her had been cleansed of desperation and depression. Now there was only love, pure and resplendent. And currently, without her presence, hollow.

Shutting the laptop screen, he forced himself to return to bed. The sheets were rumpled and cool against his bare skin. He'd gotten into the habit of sleeping naked with Erin. He continued doing it, even if the velvety cotton and faint lingering scent of her left him hard. Again.

He closed his eyes and tried to sleep. It was already three a.m. He'd have to wake up in a few hours to head to campus. She would be in class, completely untouchable. Why had he agreed to this separation again? No, he'd insisted on it. Idiot. Something about being careful in the homestretch. He wasn't sure. He couldn't think with his dick throbbing and full. Jesus.

He slid a hand to his heavy erection, gingerly rubbing the sensitive flesh. He should take care of this. No big deal. It hadn't been, before Erin. Now his dick protested the callused palm, which suddenly felt like sandpaper. His dick wanted the soft, smooth lushness of Erin's body, but too damn bad.

Just get it over with.

Shuttling a hand up and down, he let his eyes fall shut. He imagined that, instead of a dark room, sunlight streamed through. Instead of tangled sheets, a damp towel lay slack around his hips. And instead of an empty house, Erin had arrived to clean his house that day months ago.

He would never really know if he had secretly, subconsciously planned for her to find him, naked and touching himself. He would never know if she had gone to his room looking for him, instead of working downstairs as she normally did, because she wanted it too. But he had been utterly exposed that day, and when he'd realized she had seen him climaxing and calling her name, he'd been mortified—and beyond aroused.

Of course, then he'd been more worried about scaring her off. But now, alone and wearing nothing but fantasies, he allowed himself to imagine it differently. He hadn't climaxed, but instead had noticed her while he'd still been fucking his fist. She hadn't run away; no, she'd come closer with a wicked tilt of her lips. She'd knelt between his legs on the bed and taken over with her hands, her mouth.

When he tried to protest, she shook her head and pressed his hands to the bed. *Stay still.* He shuddered but obeyed, suffering in ecstasy while she teased him. In reality, his own hand delivered a swift and biting caress to his pulsing dick, but in his fantasy, it was her hot mouth, her nimble hands, and most of all, the knowing glint in her eyes that pushed him over, sending warm ejaculate across the plane of his stomach.

As he caught his breath in the aftermath, the splatter from his climax cooled into a decidedly unsexy substance. He sighed and retreated to the restroom to wipe his body clean. He was going to have long, hard days until he could see her again. And when he did? Well, tying her to the bed was looking better and better. Days and months and years of pleasure. Forever of it.

CHAPTER FOUR

ERIN

Three days until the end of semester

THE HALLWAYS CHANGED in the minutes before class started. Stragglers who had been chatting after their last class cleared out. Latecomers rushed to find their rooms before the ancient bell rang. This building held mostly graduate courses. There was, of course, no official penalty for tardiness to class, but showing respect was part of the game.

At least, it was for most of the professors.

Blake didn't seem to play the same game. He never seemed to mind when folks rushed in late or had to leave early for something. He never acted like a question was stupid or insulted someone for disagreeing with him. If she had any doubt, she would know it now—he was the real deal. A man of integrity.

He wasn't going to tell her she wasn't good enough. He already knew her mom cleaned houses, and he was fine with it. He hadn't been prejudiced—no, that had been her. Internalizing the hurt and betrayal her mother had received, distrusting those with more money, more power. But she wasn't her mother, and Blake would never hurt her.

The reminder of her mother formed an uneasy knot in her stomach. It had been a while since her mom had called. Not an unheard of amount of time, but unease niggled at her. And the last time they'd spoken, her mother had seemed distant on the phone. She'd mentioned being in pain, something about her knees bothering her. Was it worse than she'd let on? Erin stepped into an alcove and hit the speed dial. It rang five times before going to voicemail.

"Hey, Mom, it's me. Just calling to check in and see how you're feeling. You're okay, right? Call me back."

Frowning, she slipped the phone into her bag. She'd have to try again later.

Slipping into the classroom, she waved to her friend Bailey as she made her way to the back of the room. The two of them were always the quietest ones during class discussions. She refrained from speaking too much so as to avoid giving away anything about her and Blake.

Sometimes she would contribute under her breath. Bailey would hear and respond just as softly. Once, she'd worried he had a crush on her, but he never asked her out or made a move at all, which relieved her.

"How was it?" she asked, referring to the visit from his mother this past weekend. He'd mentioned it in the past few classes with typical young bachelor dread.

"Great. She declared my house a pig sty and decided to stay at a hotel."

She snorted. "Well, what can she expect with three roommates?"

"Exactly what I said. Though I might have made it worse before she showed up."

"Bailey!"

"I couldn't have survived, Erin. She's planning on staying in town until the final scores come back. That's almost a week."

"Three days," she corrected grimly. Three more days until she and Blake were together again. "Then we're both free."

He gave her a curious look. "Do you know where you're going yet? What you're going to do?"

"I have a few applications out," she admitted. It felt strange to confide in Bailey and not Blake, but maybe it was better this way. She had applied to places near Blake's house, and she didn't want to imply promises she couldn't keep regarding moving in with him.

"Cross your fingers for me," she said. "What about you? Any plans?"

"Actually I was thinking of doing a tour of Europe. Find myself or something like that, before I have to decide which major I actually want to use."

"That sounds awesome. Both the traveling and the double major. I didn't know you'd done that. What are they?"

He blushed. "I got the idea from Ayn Rand. To learn about physics and philosophy. The physical world and metaphysical one. Combined, it's everything there is to know."

She grinned. "That sounds ambitious."

"Yes, well, now that I have the degrees, I'm sure the enlightenment is coming any day." He rolled his eyes in a sweet, self-deprecating way. "I'll just hold my breath."

Her attention was snagged as Blake entered the room. He looked fresh and happy. She tore her gaze away to refocus on Bailey.

He was looking at her strangely. "Don't let him slip away."

She blinked, her smile faltering. "Who?"

"You know who." His gaze flicked to the front of the room, where Blake fielded a question from two animated students.

"How did you—?"

He shrugged, his smile wry. "I would have made a move myself, but it was clear you were taken."

Her breath caught. "Bailey…"

"It's okay, Erin. Just…hang onto it, that's all. If he makes you happy. That's all there is. Being happy."

She swallowed. Her smile felt fragile—and already cracked. "Is that your advice as a physicist or a philosopher?"

"Both."

In a move so familiar she ached with it, Blake flipped the chair around and sat down facing the class. His elbows rested on the back of the chair, his wrists hung loosely. The whole room became quiet with respect well-earned.

He'd done such an amazing job. So much more than she could have imagined. He was intelligent and thoughtful and passionate, yes. She'd known that much. But his real strength had been teasing out *their* intelligence. Testing their thoughts and bringing their passion to the fore.

She was going to miss this class. The energy, the way she lit up when he spoke. The way *he* lit up when he really got into it, as if he'd found himself in the sharing of knowledge.

"Today is our last meeting," he said. "So I want to run down the schedule real quick. Your final papers are due to me at midnight. Because of the abbreviated schedule for summer, I have to turn in grades in a very short amount of time, so don't be late. It won't be a question of my giving you an extension or extra credit. Once I turn in grades next week, even I can't change them. Got it?"

A round of nods and some shifty eyes followed his pronouncement, probably by folks who'd be up late working on the paper. Anticipation strummed through her. The grades were due on the same day as her thesis...the same day as the Faculty Ball.

And the next day she'd get to see Blake again.

"Today is our last meeting," he repeated, his manner turning thoughtful, "so I also want to tell you how incredibly impressed I am with you all. How grateful I am that you put up with me as I bumbled my way through my first class. How much I believe in each of you."

Erin bit her lip to keep from sighing out loud.

Glancing around, she saw embarrassed flushes and bright eyes. God, he'd turned a classroom full of cynical co-eds into an after school special.

She loved him. She was in awe of him.

"Albert Einstein once said that imagination is more important than knowledge. I'm sitting up here, as your professor, because of things I know. That's knowledge. You're sitting in front of me because you have the initiative, the ambition, and the creativity to do something with it. That's imagination. What you have is far more important than what I can do up here. You trump me."

A poignant quiet rang out in the room.

"Can anyone tell me what Einstein's Nobel Prize was for?"

Everyone was silent. She wasn't sure. It was in physics, she knew that much. Her science education was limited to ping-pong ball experiments in her high school AP class. But Bailey had majored in physics. She snuck a glance at him.

Bailey wore a reluctant look. He never spoke in class, but it seemed he couldn't let the question go unanswered. "The photoelectric effect, which led to the discovery of quantum physics."

"Yes, that's right," Blake said. "Can you tell us what it means in layman's terms?"

Bailey leaned forward. Clearly this subject interested him. It drew him into the discussion he'd so long avoided, and in a sudden flash of insight, Erin wondered if Blake had done this on purpose. The one student who'd resisted participation, besides her, and Blake had hit upon a subject important to him.

"In the old days," Bailey explained, "matter was made of particles and light was made up of waves. But during experiments with ultraviolet light, they determined that wave theory didn't account for certain behavior. Einstein was the one who suggested that light was, in fact, particles as well."

Blake nodded. "There were physicists and scholars with full knowledge of how things worked. Knowledge wasn't enough. It would never have been enough to make that leap. Only imagination was enough. Bailey, how can you tell whether something is a particle or a wave?"

"You can't. If you measure it as a particle, it's a particle. If you measure it as a wave, it's a wave."

"In fact, it goes a step further. If you want to examine an electron, you must basically throw a photon at it, thus changing its course. It's called the observer effect. Science 101. And we're scientists too, just on the social scale. Can you think of an example of the observer effect in the social sciences?"

"When reporters embed themselves in a military unit," someone offered. "That unit might behave differently under scrutiny, thus affecting the outcome of their missions."

"Excellent. What else?"

Another raised his hand briefly before speaking. "Kids have to take standardized tests in school. At first it was to measure their progress, but now teachers have to teach specifically for the test."

"Yes, right. The act of measuring has affected the primary source."

"The help," Erin offered blandly. "The presence of a maid might change the behavior of the household members."

His lip twitched. "Very much so." He paused, looking distant. "This is the last day of class, so I need to tell you that you are all activists. Each one of you and every person you pass on the street. Even if you sit back and hope someone else will fix the problem. You can't ignore the problems in the world. Your inaction *is* action. If you *see* the problem, if you're observing it, you're already having an effect. The only question is what that effect will be."

"I've always been a fan of throwing photons, myself," one boy quipped, and there were snorts and chuckles around the room.

Blake smiled, but it was tinged with sadness. "This is our last class. And so what I want to tell you, the most important lesson I can teach you, is to respect the people who disagree with you. They are the ones who challenge you. And even if you are right, so are they. If you measure it as a particle, it's a particle. If you measure it as a wave, it's a wave. Both sides are right. Respect that. Learn from it. Find the common ground, because that's where the true answer lies."

Chapter Five

Erin

The end of semester

ERIN'S THESIS DEFENSE took two hours, longer than she'd been expecting.

Everyone on the panel had asked thoughtful, curious questions about her research, her assumptions, her methods. She had expected to feel interrogated, or worse, accused. Like one of the women who spoke up, only to be faced with society's ridicule. Instead she'd stood in front of these professors, these experts and thought leaders, and felt like an equal.

It was heady and terrifying.

Grades were in, and the panel would make their recommendation. She wouldn't find out the results until later; however, she wasn't worried about either. She had worked her ass off on both her paper for Blake's class and her thesis.

She knew in her bones that they were good.

Melinda caught up with her in the hallway.

"Erin, can I speak with you a moment?"

Dread sank in her stomach. The woman had been very quiet during the defense. She had asked a few questions which were direct but not cruel.

Erin had hoped that would be the end of it.

Taking a fortifying breath, she turned to face the other woman.

Melinda grimaced slightly, as if she knew about Erin's discomfort—and felt bad about it. "You were great in there. I'm serious. Your research was stronger than a number of doctoral papers I've seen. And the topic is important."

"Oh, thank you," she said cautiously, waiting for the other shoe to drop. Waiting for the "but..." that would bring it all crashing down. Maybe she would expose her relationship with Blake after all. Even though he hadn't touched her in weeks, if anyone asked questions, she would tell the truth.

Melinda sighed, leading her through the doors into a small courtyard. "I need to apologize for the things I said the other day. It wasn't right, and I knew it, but..." A small laugh. "I guess, of all people, you would understand what I lost. Who I lost. I wasn't thinking straight."

Erin ducked her head. "I thought you were the one who left him."

"Yes," she admitted. "I'm not proud of that. But he wasn't like this before. He was withdrawn and angry, and I wasn't sure he'd ever go back to the way he was. His scars were part of it, but you and I both know they go deeper than that."

Erin pursed her lips. She wasn't about to perform a psychological analysis on Blake, especially with this woman as her partner. Regret or not, Melinda had no right to him.

"Can I go now?"

Melinda laughed softly. "I can't fault you for that. If he had to end up with someone else, at least it's someone who truly cares about him."

"I do." And I'm ready to be with him, without having to hide.

"Well, I won't keep you. I just wanted to apologize and tell you that I won't be a problem from now on, between you and him."

Erin weighed the sincerity of her words and found she believed them. Still, she wasn't inclined to be generous with the memory of her humiliation still strong. The woman had basically accused her of being a prostitute. "I accept your apology, but just so you know...you couldn't have caused a problem between me and him. Not anymore."

Glossy lips twisted into a wry smile. "You're probably right about that. He's loyal. I think you did the right thing not telling him about his father."

Her throat clenched. "What do you mean?"

"A senator from upstate? It wasn't hard to put the pieces together. Blake may not like everything his father's done, but he wouldn't allow anyone to hurt the people he loves."

It felt like serrated saws moved through her chest, because she knew it was true. Blake had both integrity and loyalty. Erin didn't want to know which one would win. She also didn't want to make him choose between his family and herself.

So she had left Senator Morris's name out of her thesis.

She burned with desire to see him right now, to kiss and make love to him until the world outside faded to black. To reassure herself that he was still the man she knew and loved. However, he had the Faculty Ball tonight. She could survive one more night without him, couldn't she? It would be a near thing.

They'd be together again tomorrow.

They'd have forever together…tomorrow.

And he's mine.

The force of the words shocked her. At least she managed not to say them out loud, as she made her escape from Melinda. But privately, her tenderness for him, her possession surged impossibly strong. He was hers. Hers to love. Hers to keep.

At her apartment, she found Courtney packing.

The room had disappeared between a mountain of clothes. A huge piece of luggage sat open and empty. From the haggard look on Courtney's face, things had not been going well.

Erin paused at the door. "What happened?"

"What happened is that Derek and I are going on a trip." She frowned, examining a pair of puffy pants. "And I have nothing to wear."

"Where is he taking you, the tundra?"

"Close. Colorado. We're going to do some late skiing. He's booked a suite in a lodge. Isn't that the sweetest gesture?"

"But you hate the cold."

"Yes, he must have forgotten that."

"And aren't you afraid of heights?"

"Right. I should be okay if I stick to the bunny slopes, right?"

Erin had no idea. Skiing had certainly never been part of her family vacations, which had mostly consisted of her mom and her at the beach for a weekend. She suspected even a baby slope would be big enough to terrify the girl who shut her eyes when they crossed a bridge.

"Will you hate me if I say this is a bad idea?"

"No. Because you're right, and it is a bad idea."

"But you're doing it anyway."

"I love that you get me. I mean, really understand me. You're a great friend."

"Hmm," Erin said, wondering where this was going.

"Like the kind of friend who would help me pack and figure out what to bring."

Erin stared dubiously at the mountains of clothes. Tank tops, miniskirts. They had their work cut out for them, but it was just the distraction she needed. She didn't want to think about Blake or his father. She didn't want to wonder if she'd done the right thing. Blake would be at the Faculty Ball right now, and the fact that Erin couldn't attend as his date only highlighted the separation, made it feel so much deeper and longer than one more night.

"You're on," Erin said, digging into the pile.

She ended up pulling everything out of her closet, as well, matching outfits so she could look cute for their renewed relationship, as well as warm enough not to freeze to death.

Hours passed, and Erin lost herself in the chatter with her good friend. She would miss this when she moved in with Blake. Except she hadn't agreed to that.

So when Courtney asked her about re-upping the lease, Erin said quickly, "I'm not moving in with him," and immediately blushed. As soon as she said the words, she knew they were a lie.

Courtney raised her eyebrows. "Want to bet?"

She knew the truth. Even Blake probably knew it was inevitable. Everyone except Erin understood. She'd put him off. *Not now, later. We'll talk about it later.*

Now was later, and God, she wanted to be with him. Night and day. Forever and ever, amen. *This must be serious*, he had said in a teasing tone. With the worry of school behind her, she was damned serious.

"Okay, I might move in with him. And maybe even...I don't know, marry him. Does that sound crazy?"

"Of course you're going to marry him. See, when you find a boy who you like, and who you want to have sex with, you have to do the right thing by him. Otherwise he starts to wonder if you're just using him for his body."

Erin huffed a laugh. Blake loved when she

used him for his body. But that was a good idea. Maybe she could pop the question. It would be worth it just to see the look on his face. Not right now, but soon. Maybe then she wouldn't feel so guilty about not answering him right away about moving in. Then she might not feel this gnawing emptiness at being apart.

She helped Courtney stuff the luggage full and then sat on it so they could zipper it shut. They loaded her friend's car together and hugged before she got inside.

Courtney frowned. "Sorry to abandon you so soon after your defense. I should have taken you out for drinks to celebrate. And I made you pack with me. I'm a shitty friend."

"I don't mind, sweetie. You have fun. And bring back lots of stories."

"Always. And I'm still taking you out for drinks when I get back. We'll get a cab together and get totally wasted."

Sadness clamped Erin's stomach as she waved goodbye, and she realized that at least part of her hesitancy was leaving Courtney. She'd been an amazing friend. They would still be friends, but the roommate bond ran deeper. They talked all the time. They knew each other's secrets. Soon it would be her and Blake. Yes, she wanted that, but she would still miss her friend.

Her cellphone trilled from inside the apartment. She almost sprinted to answer it. Her mother hadn't returned a call in days now, and Erin was beyond worried. The number on the screen wasn't her mother's. Disappointment tightened her stomach.

"Hello?"

"Hello, is this Erin Rodriguez?"

The officiousness of the tone drew her to full alert. "Yes, that's me."

The woman proceeded to introduce herself as the head nurse of the urgent care ward at Lakota County General Hospital. A wave of dizziness swept over Erin, but she gripped the phone tightly and held on.

The nurse's voice was sympathetic. "I'm calling to inform you that your mother was admitted into our care after suffering a major heart attack."

Fear gripped her. A heart attack? Her mother was an older woman, but she was strong and healthy. Or she had been. Oh God. The world lost focus as she took in the rest of the information. Yes, her mother was alive and in recovery. No, she couldn't speak to her mother right now— she was sleeping, a side effect of the medicines she was on. Yes, Erin would be able to visit her mother if she arrived before visiting hours were over.

Erin's thoughts came wild and unordered, matching the state of her room.

Her clothes were strewn across the floor and bed. She grabbed a few tops and a pair of jeans and stuffed them into her backpack. In a sort of trance, she walked to her car and slipped her key into the ignition.

Nothing happened.

She took out her key and tried again. The engine turned over and then stalled. Her old, trusty rustbucket had finally given out and at the worst possible time. She tried three more times, but the car had well and truly given up.

Feeling sick, she struggled to focus.

The most important thing was to get to her mother. She could deal with the repairs later. But how could she get there? The drive was four hours away. The one time she'd had to take the transit bus from her city to the college, after Doug had left her, the trip had taken twice that long from all the stops in between.

Her mind spun, running through all the options she had and coming up empty. She didn't mind being alone, not really, but times like now, it did hurt. Except she wasn't alone.

Blake. He would know the answer.

He'd asked her to find him if she needed him, and she did.

She suddenly couldn't wait to be near him, to lean on his strength and feel his embrace. Any attempt to shield herself had been in vain. She was already his, under his domain and beholden—and it was exactly where she wanted to be. It had nothing to do with where her body resided. In times of fear and worry, her heart turned to him.

BLAKE

BLAKE TOOK A swig of his cocktail. The sweet syrup clung to his tongue and the liquor burned his throat, but drinking still beat talking. He'd already had to tell the story of his scars twice, and he wasn't eager to tell it a third time.

He gave a scrubbed version, of course.

The real thing wasn't fit for the string quartet or the gowns of the Faculty Ball, though that fact didn't deter them from asking. His scars were so *fascinating*, they said, as if it were the best compliment—and to a group of strident intellectuals, perhaps it was.

They took his refusals as modesty first and rudeness second, until he'd resignedly told some softened, civilian-friendly account of what had happened.

"There you are." The slurred words came from behind him. Jeremy Mosely, the dean of his department and his boss for the semester, approached unsteadily.

Blake wished he could stand the signature cocktail well enough to get drunk. As it was he still nursed the first one. "Jeremy. Good seeing you."

He grinned. "Hah, I know you've been avoiding me."

Even sloshed, the man was smart. "Sorry. I've been a little distracted."

"Not too distracted. I heard your semester went great." He looked smug. "I know you're thinking about renewing your contract. I'll give you a few days to think about it before I do the hard sell on you."

Damn, the man was right again. He had been considering it...once he and Erin were settled. Once she moved in with him. *If* she moved in with him. He took another drink, wincing at the sickly sweet flavor.

"Disgusting, I know," Jeremy continued. "I have a secret stash, if you're up for it."

"I was thinking of heading out soon."

It was ten o'clock. Not exactly late, but he wanted to get to bed at a reasonable time and see Erin in the morning. He had a full suite of activities planned for her that would require most of the hours in the day and most of the surfaces in his house. They had so much time to make up for. His body thrummed in restless, unsatisfied longing. *Soon soon soon.*

"No, come on. The night's still young."

"Maybe, but I'm not."

"Please, you're the youngest guy in the room. A couple of guys were going to the faculty basement. Bet you never heard about that when you were a student here."

Curiosity nudged him. "Okay, what's the faculty basement? And if you tell me whips and chains, I'm definitely not going with you."

Jeremy snorted. "Well, it's going to sound boring compared to that. It's a recreation room for professors. Sort of a *members only* type of thing. There's nice furniture, good liquor, and a pool table that's been here since the university's inception."

"How did I never know about this?"

"Because you weren't tenured."

"I'm still not tenured."

"Call it a sales pitch. You can come see what

you'd be missing."

"Hmm." He'd always had a soft spot for the school, ever since he was a wide-eyed freshman. It amused him to realize there were new things to discover in a place he'd been for so many years. Blake eyed the room, catching a few curious glances his way as he did.

People looked away quickly. They didn't want to be caught staring.

Anywhere had to be better than this. "Let's go."

Jeremy rounded up a couple of tenured professors that Blake had met before and headed two buildings over and downstairs into the basement. He had promised Erin, and himself, that he would try to rejoin society. That meant more than clocking in and out of a job, whatever it was. It meant the rare social occasion like this. He looked forward to the time Erin would join him at parties like this. If he was going to sneak out of the party early and into some dimly lit recess, he'd far rather be doing it with her.

Inside the faculty basement, there were thick leather armchairs that made him feel like wearing a smoking jacket. The other guys started up a game on the green felt pool table in the corner, but Jeremy came to sit by him. There was something he wanted to talk about, but Blake could be patient. He accepted the offered glass of whiskey and a cigar.

Jeremy settled in opposite him and was quiet for a moment. "I know you and Melinda used to be an item."

Blake raised his eyebrows. "What of it?"

"Just wondering if there's anything still between you two."

Christ. First his goddamn battle scars had to be story time for the group, now he'd been lured by alcohol to talk about his past lovelorn humiliation. Being back in society was a laugh a minute.

"No. It's over. Very much so."

"Good to hear it."

Blake raised his eyebrows. "Why, is there some sort of policy against intradepartmental dating?"

Jeremy laughed shortly. "I hope not. I was thinking of asking her out."

"Oh." Well, that put a new spin on their shared nightcap.

A sideways glance. "So, what do you think?"

"About you and Melinda? I think nothing about that. Whatsoever."

"You must think something. You think she's

too hot for me?"

"The thought hadn't crossed my mind." At least he could be honest about that.

"Well, come on. Give me something here. If you're not trying to get back together, help a fellow out. I know she's still talking to you, too."

Hmm. Melinda wouldn't spill on him and Erin, not anymore, but it would be best not to stir this pot too strongly. He pretended to think about it. And then he actually did think about it. Mosely was a smart guy, and he seemed ambitious enough. Melinda could help support him. Blake was no matchmaker, but it wasn't a bad setup.

He shrugged. "What the hell do I know?"

"Thanks, man. Real encouraging."

A surprised laugh burst from him. He supposed he really had been out of the loop for too long. He'd forgotten how to be a friend.

"Shit. Sorry." He leaned forward, staring into his drink. The sight of amber-colored liquid reminded him of his morning with Erin a few weeks ago, and God, what a morning that had been. He couldn't wait to repeat it.

Preferably every morning from now on.

Forever. The thought should have scared him, being a standard fare red-blooded male. Especially in light of what had happened with Melinda. But the thought of *not forever*, of losing her, was the real threat. He would make it official and ask her to marry him, but he might scare her away. Asking her to move in had already been a big step, and she hadn't said yes yet. She was still young. He felt vaguely guilty tying her down.

Not guilty enough to stop.

Besides, he knew better than anyone that putting a ring on her finger wouldn't guarantee anything. It hadn't with Melinda. All he and Erin had to offer each other was one day at a time.

For the first time, he thought it might be enough.

"You should ask her out," he finally said. "Even if it doesn't work out, at least you'll have given it a chance. It's better than not living."

The other man studied him. "That sounds like the voice of experience."

"It is, and you were one of the people who helped bring me back. I owe you for that."

Jeremy clapped him on the shoulder. "Then come to work with me. A tenured position. The board will approve it in a heartbeat."

Ah, it seemed they'd arrived at the hard sell portion of the evening. What the hell, he'd known what his answer would be. Teaching was too damn fun.

So was living, he had found out the hard way.

A swig of the expensive liquor. It went down smooth. "Then I accept. Oh, and by the way, can I ask you a favor? Could you send me a copy of the doctorate theses this year?"

"Sure. A little light reading?"

He allowed himself a small smile. "I like to know what the next generation is thinking about. And include the undergraduate senior theses while you're at it."

He really did want to know what the next generation was thinking about.

Reading Erin's thesis would be a bonus.

CHAPTER SIX

ERIN

FRANTIC AND DIZZY with worry, Erin redialed Blake's cell phone.

He wasn't picking up at home either, but she took a chance that he'd fallen asleep quickly. The cab fare was thirty dollars just to get from her apartment to his empty, dark house. *Damn.* The Faculty Ball had ended at eleven and it was already midnight, so where was he?

She had a flash of panic. What if he were hurt? What if he'd had something to drink and he'd been driving and... no. *Calm down.* That was the kind of thing that happened in movies, like in *An Affair to Remember.* Blake was fine. If he did drink, he was probably waiting somewhere until he sobered up enough to drive.

His office, she realized.

He might even be there to finish up paperwork or clear out his books. It was the type of thing he might do, avoiding socializing under the pretense of some work task. Especially if things had gone poorly. Damn, now she was worried about that too. Her worry was strung up tight like the string of a bow, pulled back and ready to fire. If only she had a damn target.

She returned to the waiting cab and shut the door. "Campus, please."

"You got it."

The fare ticked higher as they retraced their steps back toward the university. It was going to take everything she had in her wallet to pay the fare. She'd check the office. He *had* to be there. Because if he wasn't, she had no idea where he could be, and she had no other plan.

"Any chance you guys go out of town?" she asked the cab driver.

"Sure. Where you headed?" When she told him the name of her hometown, he plugged it into his GPS. "That'd be a flat rate trip. Looks like $450 to get you there."

She almost groaned. Four hundred dollars? Her bank account had that much—but barely. She'd wipe it clean and have nothing left to fix her car with when she got back.

When they arrived at the campus checkpoint, she paid him, hesitantly adding a tip from her meager stash. If she ended up taking the bus, she'd use up the last twenty in her purse and it would be tomorrow by the time she arrived. The cab drove away, leaving her in a cloud of smog. She didn't have a ride to the bus station now either.

She was running out of options.

The buildings appeared deserted as she walked quickly by.

Moonlight bounced off the pale stone surfaces. She had been here a few times at night for study groups, but now, after the summer semester had ended, no one lingered. She had no idea where on campus the Faculty Ball was being held, but that was probably for the best. Even desperate, she knew better than to crash a party and expose their relationship.

The wide metal doors she normally used to get inside that building were locked. She circled around and found a side door open. Pushing it open, she blinked into the darkness. It didn't take long to figure out that his office was also dark, and empty. He wasn't here.

It had been a thin hope anyway.

Feeling a knot of fear for her mother, she wandered outside and sat down on a bench. The grounds were picturesque on the historical campus. Gorgeous lawns and famous statues. She didn't see any of it. Ancient oak trees and architectural features blurred in front of her.

This was her nightmare.

Knowing her mother needed her and being unable to get there. Three hundred miles felt a continent away. And even once she arrived, she wouldn't be able to do anything useful. She wouldn't be able to fix her mom's heart.

She wouldn't be able to pay the medical bills.

Helpless.

A trill of laughter from around the corner caught her attention. Then a male voice answered. Damn, she recognized that voice. Wiping her eyes, she sat up straighter. *Please, let him walk past me.* Tonight luck had abandoned her completely.

Her old boyfriend Doug wandered nearer, half dragging an unsteady girl.

Other voices bounced off the walls farther away, and she knew they were his friends. Doug always preferred to travel with a group, even when he was with his girlfriend—which had been her, once upon a time.

"Erin? Is that you?"

She tried to keep her voice from wavering. "Hey. What's up?"

"What's up is I'm happy to see you. God-damn, Erin Rodriguez." He sounded genuinely happy to see her, and not even drunk. She wondered if he had drawn the designated driver short stick. He turned to the girl on his arm. "Go join the others. I'll catch up in a minute." She wandered in the direction of the voices, her stilettos sticking in the lawn.

Knowledge pierced Erin's worried haze. "Wait, what are you doing here?" she asked Doug. "Don't tell me you came back for grad school?"

He snorted. "Nah. It's one of my friend's brother's birthday so we hit the bars nearby. I'm just along to keep the little kiddos from hurting themselves."

"You're the chaperone?" she asked, her voice wry. "What is this world coming to?"

"That's what I said, but according to them, I've lost my edge. I'm all responsible and grown up and boring now."

"Welcome to the club," she said dryly.

He sat down on the same bench, reclining on the opposite corner. "So are you going to tell me what's wrong?"

"Nothing's wrong."

He gave her a look of reprimand. "We dated for a year and a half. Which, for me, was practically a lifelong commitment. I think I can still tell when you're upset."

Strangely enough, she could read his emotions as well.

His hair was shorter now, almost a buzz cut instead of the floppy hair she'd loved to run her fingers through. He seemed taller somehow, though it didn't seem possible he would have grown. His posture was relaxed but expectant.

She read his body language, his face, even without having seen him for years. Familiarity was a strange thing, muted with time but never turned off.

"My mom had a heart attack," she admitted. "I was trying to get back there tonight, but my car broke down and then…" She didn't really want to get into the specifics of her roommate being out of town and her secret boyfriend being a professor here. She shook her head. "It just isn't working out. Maybe I can get a mechanic to repair my car in the morning."

"On a Sunday morning? Not likely. Let me drive you back."

She stared at him. "Back home, I mean. The four-hour drive."

"I know what you meant. I'll take you there."

"I can't put you out that way."

He looked away. "I owe you that ride anyway, even if it's in the opposite direction. I've always felt bad for ditching you. That was a real dick move."

She opened her mouth to reassure him. *No, it's okay. I understood.* But she didn't. She hadn't understood how she could have meant so little to him because of what their parents had or hadn't done. Because of something outside of her control.

Sighing, she said, "It was a long time ago."

"It's never too late to repay a debt. Let me drive you there."

Temptation tugged at her. In a manner of speaking, he did owe her this, so she wasn't just inconveniencing a stranger. And she really wanted to get home.

Was her mother awake now? Was she afraid or in pain?

Erin could only hope that the hospital care she received was expert, but what if her mother needed someone to advocate for her? Erin needed to be there, and she had no other way to go. No one else to take her. She glanced at her phone.

Still no return call from Blake.

Would he be pissed about Doug taking her? Would he suspect that she'd been cheating on him? No, she couldn't believe that. He'd understand when he found out that her mother was ill, when he heard that her car had broken down.

When he saw the twelve missed calls from her.

He had to understand. She'd make him understand.

"Okay," she said on a resigned breath. "I appreciate it. And if you want, I can drive there, so you can sleep on the way." She offered this even knowing he would refuse.

"Did I ever, in all the time you knew me, let another person drive my car?"

A reluctant smile touched her lips. "It's late. You must be tired."

"Never that tired. Not even for you, Erin."

"You always loved your car," she said with a touch of affection.

"Even more now," he promised. "This one I paid for myself."

It took almost an hour for Doug to shepherd his friends back to their place and retrieve his car from a parking lot near the clubs. She watched her phone, hoping Blake would see her missed calls. She had begun to worry about him as well, but she had to trust he was safe.

She also had to trust that he wasn't just ignoring her or off with Melinda.

Old worries couldn't touch her now. Faced

with failing her mother, with losing her, she had no energy for baseless fears. Blake was kind and loyal, and she wouldn't doubt him.

She only wished that he were here.

As Doug pulled to the curb in a sleek new Audi, she dialed Blake's number one last time. This time it didn't even ring, going straight to voicemail.

"It's me. I got a ride back, with Doug." She wasn't sure how to describe him, and she certainly didn't want to say *that guy I told you about who broke my heart.* "Don't worry about me. Everything will be fine. I'll see you when I get back."

As she stepped into the low floor of the car, she realized the assurances were more for herself than him. Everything would be fine, with her mother, and with him. With herself.

"You okay?" Doug asked, concerned.

She forced a smile. "I will be."

BLAKE

"FIFTEEN IN THE corner." The familiar thud and reverberation of his stick told him he'd shot true. The striped orange ball tipped over the lip of green felt and tumbled in.

His opponent was George Evans, professor of

Greek Archaeology. Evans shook his head. "Goddamn. Are you hustling me, Morris?"

Blake snorted. "I wish."

Though his game had definitely improved. The first shot had been embarrassing. The cue had ricocheted around the table, somehow managing to miss every single goddamn ball.

His eye had escaped the blast unscathed, but his depth perception had been affected. Something about the way the skin formed around it, or rather didn't form, made a subtle but unmistakable difference.

This was his first time playing pool since the explosion, his first time being around people in a social setting. These men, privately, were kinder than the ones who'd questioned him at the party. They made no comment on his ineptitude and still included him.

Slowly, he learned to compensate for the change. Even when he suspected the others were tired, he'd wanted to continue playing. To keep improving.

To finally learn to deal with his injuries instead of avoiding them.

He circled the table and nodded to the side pocket to signal. Bending at the waist, he lined it up. There was his usual aim, the straight line between his stick, the cue, and the glinting side of the black eight ball. But that was wrong. If he made this shot, the cue would skate past the eight ball entirely and probably end up in the corner pocket, costing him the game.

He tilted the stick a few degrees. He preferred to change his aim rather than angle his head, he'd found. Now it appeared as though the cue would hit the eight ball dead-on, sending them both in a useless arc across the table. He pulled back and made the shot.

The cue brushed the eight, changing its course enough to head for the middle. The eight ball rolled slowly into the side pocket and landed with a clink against the other balls.

"Good game," Evans said, clapping him on the shoulder. "I mean that. You're welcome to come back and kick my ass anytime. At pool, that is. I'll wipe the floor with you about Knossos anytime."

Blake chuckled. "I have no doubt."

They'd had something of a debate about the ancient Greek citadel. Blake had been less informed than his opponent, and it had felt damn good. Evans had given him a few recommendations for journal articles to read as well. There was something exhilarating about talking with someone, the connection. The energy in the room.

Evans brushed the chalk from his hands. "I'm going to head out, actually. Don't know if the missus has been calling while we've been down here. There's never any cell coverage down here. I should probably head home either way."

Blake waved him off but stayed near the pool table instead of joining the other men for a cigar. Something about Evans's words niggled at him. What if Erin had called him? He pulled out his phone, relieved to find the screen blank. No missed calls.

Then he noticed the bars were missing. No signal either. *Don't know if the missus has been calling...* Damn. These old buildings had horrible reception to start with, and they were in the basement. For all he knew, this was some sort of old bomb shelter.

He ignored the men in the corner and took the stairs up to the building.

Still nothing, and he didn't stop walking. Pushing outside, he waited impatiently for his phone to regain signal. Like the piece of dumb machinery it was, it continued to show no signal, and like the dumb outdated guy he was, he didn't know how to tell it to check again.

A sudden sense of panic overtook him.

Irrational. Erin knew where he was tonight, and they already had a plan to meet tomorrow. Still, he couldn't deny the warning bells going off inside his head. Instinct had kept him alive and relatively safe all this time. Even the painful scars were a blessing when he considered the alternative.

He'd learned to trust those damn warning bells.

He pressed the button to restart his phone, but he didn't wait for it. He strode in the direction of his car. It was late anyway, time to go, and he would apologize to the guys later for leaving so abruptly. He needed to check on Erin, to make sure she was okay. Because the bells told him something was wrong.

He was halfway to her apartment when his phone decided to buzz and beep at him. His heart dropped from his chest. Thirteen missed calls. An unlucky number, he thought uselessly. All from Erin. What could have happened? He'd missed her. He'd failed her. Grimly, he pressed the voicemail button to find out exactly how.

Chapter Seven

Erin

Erin woke up with her heart pounding.

She turned to her mother, who was sleeping peacefully, the machines beeping in steady reassurance. Someone had dimmed the lights since she'd last been awake, leaving only a soft lamp above and a soothing blue from the machine monitors. Squeezing the limp hand she held, Erin turned toward a soft scuffing sound.

A nurse gave her a sympathetic look. "I have to kick you out before the nurse shift changes. You can come back in after she's been seen by the doctor."

"Oh. Right." They had snuck her in against the official visiting hours. She was so grateful for the nurses's tired smiles and gentle words. The doctor, too, seemed kind and knowledgeable. Even the room was welcoming, more like a modern styled bedroom than a hospital room—if she didn't count the bed. At least her mother was receiving excellent medical care. Her pallor still scared Erin. Blue veins whispered beneath her skin. Her mother's eyes had fluttered open for a few minutes in the middle of the night.

"Erin," she'd murmured. "You came."

Desperate, Erin had spoken urgent words of love and apology, of regret and promises, but her mother had drifted back to sleep without another word.

Erin stood, wincing at the twinge in her back. The metal and plastic chairs were not the most comfortable for sleeping, but she wasn't about to complain. She forced a sleepy smile as she gathered up her purse and luggage.

Doug was propped up against the wall, an empty cup of coffee dangling from his fingertips. He straightened as she came out, rubbing his eyes.

"How is she?"

"I told you to go home and get some sleep," she scolded softly. "But she seems well. Stable, they said. Right now it's just the medicine keeping her sleepy, but they said it's best she doesn't move around too much anyway."

His expression was sympathetic. "How are you holding up?"

"I'm fine."

He studied her. "No offense, but you look

awful."

"Now why would that be offensive?" she asked, her voice dry.

"Sorry," he said with a small, repentant grin that had gotten him out of so much trouble. It was what had endeared him to her once, a way of making light of life. She still appreciated the sentiment, the escape of it, even if it wouldn't ever be real. Her life was about struggle and about courage—the same as Blake's. Thinking of him made her heart clench.

"It's okay." She scrubbed at her face.

Surely he was right anyway. Worry and lack of sleep probably imprinted dark shadows under eyes. Her hair felt unruly and knotted to the touch.

"You really should head home, though. I can take it from here. You don't have to wait for me either. In town, I mean. You can get back to your friends in Tanglewood."

"And leave you stranded? Again? Not likely."

She waved a hand. "I'll figure it out, now that I have time. I'm not sure how long I'll need to stay here, so there's no point in you hanging around for this. And wouldn't you miss work? You'd better drive back today."

Doug had sped on the open night roads, pulling into the hospital at four thirty in the morning. She glanced at the clock now, surprised to see it was already eight.

"No, I—" He paused, seeming at a loss for words and unusually sincere. "I want to be here. To help you, if I can. I'm not asking to start anything right now. I know it's not the time. But if sometime in the future, you and I were to be together again…"

"Doug, what about the girl you were with?"

"She's just a friend," he said. When she raised an eyebrow, he amended, "With benefits."

She shook her head. He would never change—not that she'd been waiting for that. She doubted they would have worked in the long term, even if there hadn't been the horrible situation with her mother and his parents.

He seemed to follow her line of thinking. "I'm sorry about what happened when you came. I had no idea there was a connection. And then when I found out, I panicked."

She stopped with him with a hand on his forearm. "I understand. I did my share of panicking. It was a bad situation."

He looked away. "I know your mom didn't steal," he said tightly.

It was as close to a confession as she would

ever get, and more than she deserved, really. It wasn't their fight. It never should have been their fight. It was their parents. His father and my mother. A terrible heritage that had been passed down.

Maybe they could fight it—fight the precedent, she thought, the way Blake taught in class—except they weren't together anymore. Never would be again. What she had with Blake was so much deeper than anything she'd experienced before. Deeper than she knew was possible. She wanted Doug to find that with someone else.

Neither of them deserved to settle for each other.

"I'm sorry," she said. "That won't happen."

His expression was earnest. "You don't have to decide now. I just wanted to tell you—"

Whatever he was going to tell her was cut off by sharp footfalls and a commanding masculine voice. She looked up at the counter, and like a dream, Blake was there. He spoke quickly to the nurse on duty, who pointed in Erin's direction.

Blake turned, his gaze burning bright with concern and love and something else. Something territorial that made her heart skip a beat.

"Blake," she whispered.

The space closed between them. His gaze

never left hers.

"Ah," Doug said from beside her. "I see my position here has been made redundant."

Only then did she realize that her hand was still on his arm, how it might have looked as they sat close together. How it might seem that she had accepted help from Doug.

For a bleak moment, insecurity overtook her.

Until Blake gave Doug a brief nod of acknowledgment. A sort of proprietary thanks for helping her when he'd been missing in action. It meant that she was still his.

Relief swept through her, warm and sure.

She fell into Blake's arms without understanding the mechanics of it. One moment she was sitting on the hard-backed chair, the next she was encased in a warm, solid hug and *this*, this was what she'd so desperately needed last night. Almost as much as, even more than, the ride to her hometown. She had needed his strength, his support.

"Is she okay?" he asked against her hair.

"Yes, I think—no, but there's—" And then all semblance of composure crumbled under the onslaught of his kindness. Tears sprang to her eyes, thick and hot. They wetted her cheeks and his shirt. Her breath couldn't find a rhythm; it jumped and froze in erratic disarray. The sounds she made scared even herself—choking, gasping, *sobbing* and helpless with it.

Helpless, like she'd never wanted to be. Like she was. Like she *wasn't* when he was near, because his broad embrace sheltered her. He steadied her.

It wasn't the four-hour drive that had confounded her last night as she'd frantically roamed the campus in pursuit of Blake. It was the knowledge that her mother was sick and she could do nothing to fix it. That hadn't changed when she'd arrived at the hospital, and it didn't change now that Blake was here. But he made the helplessness more bearable.

Her life was filled with opportunity, with joy.

Her research and her study. Her love for Blake. Her few but close friendships.

But even the happiest song had a low note. And in deep, rumbling disquiet, she held tightly to him, finding refuge and temporary silence in his arms.

BLAKE

THEY WEREN'T SURE what her mother would be up for eating, so Blake grabbed five different options, along with full meals for Erin and himself. All of it balanced precariously on the two-foot cafeteria tray. He stood in line behind a heavyset woman with short grey hair. When the person in front had finished paying, they both shuffled forward. The grey-haired woman set her salad bowl down beside her plastic container of pudding and a bottle of water. She fumbled in her coin purse as the young, bored-looking lady at the cash register rang up the total to just over eight bucks.

More fumbling. "I forgot…ah, something on my salad. I just need to—"

As if realizing her excuses were falling on deaf ears, she quickly piled her items back into her arms and stepped away from the cash register.

The lady at the cash register gave him an expectant look. Blake slid forward and began to lay out his items for the lady to ring up, but he kept an eye on the grey-haired woman. She did return to the salad bar and added a spoonful of ham, as if committed to the lie now.

It was clear to the cash register lady and to himself that she hadn't had the right amount of money. She surreptitiously returned the water bottle and the pudding to their proper places before returning to the end of the line.

He leaned forward and spoke to the cashier in low tones. "I'd like to leave money for the bill behind me."

Understanding lit the young woman's eyes. "I can do that."

"And if you could…" He grimaced, trying to think of a way to make it less like charity. He didn't care; he wished he could leave more, but he suspected the grey-haired woman would mind. "If you could say it was a chain, all morning, people had done it, one after the other."

The corner of her lip tipped up. "That's sweet."

He shook his head but didn't answer. It wasn't sweet or special to give away what he had in spades. It was a trust fund. Even what little he had earned as a soldier and his short stint as temporary professor was built on the back of a wealthy upbringing and no student debt. He understood his privilege, and though he enjoyed the finer things in life—like brandy and a game of pool, for example—he wouldn't make a mockery of it.

Piling the bags and drinks in his arms, he passed the gift shop.

Balloons. Damn it. Or flowers, at least. He should have brought some.

It was the hospital smell. No, just being in a mile radius. His body had broken out in a cold sweat when he'd arrived in the parking lot, and a vice had clamped his throat when he'd walked inside. Still, his step hadn't even slowed. He'd known Erin was inside. He would walk through the halls of hell for her, and he figured a hospital qualified as such.

Gritting his teeth, he took the elevator up to the seventh floor.

It had been a relief to leave for a little while. He'd driven Erin to her mother's apartment so she could shower and pick up a few necessities. The apartment was small, modest. Erin's room still held swaths of pink reminiscent of a happy and hopeful teenage girl.

It was the kitchen that had struck him most of all. His own kitchen was ridiculously large with an island and a wine fridge. This kitchen had been barely able to hold two people standing side by side. The small wedge of a countertop was covered with mail and keys and pens. There was no microwave. Whether in his family's expensive home or in the bachelor pads of his Army buddies, there was always a microwave. Here there was simply no room for one.

No TV dinners. He imagined a teenaged Erin

cooking something small and light on the stovetop—soup or noodles. Not a bad life, but it was a splash of cold water on his face to see how differently she'd grown up.

In the hallway, the ceiling was weighted down by something unknown, turned yellow and black. The toilet in the bathroom actually tilted at an angle. The whole apartment was falling down, in shambles, but his thoughts kept returning to that kitchen. An old magnetic picture frame held a picture of a childhood Erin with a huge grin and no front teeth. He imagined her pride in her home, her mother. He imagined someone ridiculing her, finding that weakness and using it to twist the knife.

He understood better why she had doubted them as a couple, what she'd doubted in him—and herself. *She might judge you,* Erin said about her mother, but what she'd really meant was that she herself had judged him. Ironically, his biggest fear, his face, his scars, had been nothing to her. Not even a hurdle. She'd been worried about status, about money, and he couldn't care less. He'd rather give it away, give it to *her,* than let it stand between them. The barriers keeping her from him were crumbling now, slipping under their own weight.

After she'd had a chance to shower and change, they'd returned to the hospital, where she had rushed upstairs and he'd lingered downstairs to grab lunch. His footsteps slowed as he approached the hospital room. *Nervous about something?* he mocked himself. It appeared no matter how old he got, meeting the parents would always hold uncertainty.

And, he had to admit, these were hardly ideal circumstances.

Knocking shortly on the door, he pushed inside.

The woman who must be Erin's mother struggled with a pillow, sitting up in her hospital bed. Her skin was dark with age spots, lined from smiling and frowning and living, but she looked so much like the woman he loved he felt sure he could have recognized the relation if he'd passed her on the street.

Erin was nowhere to be seen. After a moment's hesitation, he set the food down and went to help her. Making a small soothing sound, he tucked the pillow behind her and helped her lean back. She calmed under his slight touch, and he withdrew quickly. Not quickly enough.

"I remember you," she said without opening her eyes. Her voice was thick with exhaustion and probably pain. She was still alert enough to remember him.

Then again it was hard to forget his face.

Her hair was darker than Erin's, her face more weathered, but he could see the resemblance in the shape of her nose and the set of her mouth. He could see the woman that Erin would become as the years passed like pages in a book.

"We met earlier. I'm Blake." Erin had insisted on introducing him this morning, but her mother had been too drowsy from the medicine to register much.

"You're her boyfriend. The one she didn't tell me about."

Boyfriend. Is that what he was? The word felt too youthful for how he felt about Erin. Too temporary, as if they might break up. Though isn't that what happened? They had been apart for weeks because he wanted it that way. Because he wanted to do the right thing. Now he cursed himself for making them separate. "That's me," he said.

"Why didn't she tell me?"

Oh, he had plenty of guesses and none that he would say out loud. Starting with the age difference between them and ending with the fact that he was the professor in her final summer semester. "We haven't been seeing each other that long."

"Long enough. I saw the way you looked at her. You love her."

His chest panged. "Yes, ma'am."

"Don't *ma'am* me. You're too old for that, and I'm not old enough."

He allowed a small smile. The habit came from the military, not as any particular thought about her age or his. "Sorry."

She peeked an eye open at him. "Why was she hiding you? There must be something wrong. And don't tell me your scars. I wouldn't even have known if she'd mentioned you over the phone. Are you married?"

"No."

"A criminal?"

"Definitely not."

She made a *humph* sound. "Your watch looks expensive."

It had been a gift from his father, sent in the mail since they hardly saw each other. Especially since the accident. He had always looked like his dad. Not anymore. He cleared his throat. "Erin thought you wouldn't like it that my family's wealthy."

Silence. Then, "She was right. I don't like it."

"I'd like to set your mind at ease, if possible."

"Well, I hope you don't think you're going to throw your money around and get what you want." Dark eyes pierce him. "Or that you can hurt her because you're rich."

The only thing he wanted, he already had in the form of her daughter. Did twenty bucks in the cafeteria line count as throwing it around?

"No." He bit his tongue to keep *ma'am* from coming out. It wasn't a slight to her age, just a sign of respect that had been drilled into him in the military. "I would never hurt Erin."

"Or making demands on her—"

"Of course not," he cut in.

"Trying to control her. Make her wear what you want and put her hair up. Parade her in front of your rich friends and then cheat on her behind her back."

"Absolutely not," he said, his voice hard. He wanted to reassure this woman, but he would not be responsible for the sins of a thousand men before him.

"Well."

"Well," he repeated. "I assured her that I'd win you over with my charm. Since I don't have any charm, we'll have to come to an understanding instead."

She paused. "Are you threatening me?"

"I would never presume to." At least partly because he had nothing to threaten her with. In fact, he wanted to get along with her, he hoped to. But he wasn't going to let anyone get between him and Erin, not even the woman who'd raised her.

Her expression was mildly pissed off. And amused. He'd seen that exact smile on Erin, and it meant he was off the hook. Of course, that didn't prove anything.

Erin liked him a lot better than this woman did.

She managed to look intimidating from her supine position. "It's no business of mine what's in your bank account, but if you hurt her, I will find you."

He let the threat hang in the air. She was short and slight. At a disadvantage financially and socially. There was nothing she could do to him, and they both knew it, but the intensity, the *worry* in her eyes squeezed a fist around his heart. He understood how much she cared for her daughter. He appreciated that she'd raised her to be strong, and smart, and confident.

Now that was his job. His responsibility, his privilege.

"Yes, ma'am," he said, because she'd given him an order and he swore to follow it. He would have done it anyway. Nothing was more important to him than Erin's safety and happiness. But if it set her mind at ease, he let his resolve show in his eyes. She studied him—his direct gaze, his disfigured skin. She didn't flinch, but then he already knew Erin had come from tough stock. They had seen the darker side of life.

"You'll do," she finally said.

It was faint praise, but it would have to be enough.

Now they needed to make sure she was discharged and healthy. He also needed to speak privately with Erin, to somehow make it up to her that he hadn't been around when she needed him. He had a full day ahead of him, basically.

Turning to the plastic bags, he began to pull out options. "We have Jello. Yogurt with granola topping. Tapioca pudding. What's your poison?"

She stared at him, unimpressed. Wordlessly, he found the container with his own loaded cheeseburger and flipped it open. The aroma of fries filled the hospital room.

With a relieved sigh, she accepted it. "You and I just might get along after all."

ERIN

THE COUNTY HOSPITAL was an old building that, if Erin were honest, was better suited to a prison than a hospital. Its rectangular shape bled inward with concentric rectangular hallways. She stood on the outmost ring, where thin, barred windows drew afternoon light onto the grey rubber floors.

"Ms. Rodriguez."

Dr. Parkins had grey hair, an ever-present clipboard, and a kind smile. What the building lacked in charm, the people made up for with their thoughtful care for her mother.

"Is my mom okay?"

"Yes, definitely. I've just been in to see her. Her condition is improving and we're moving forward to the recovery phase."

Relief swept through her. Her mother had seemed good during lunch, even making light conversation with Blake, but she was glad to have it confirmed.

"That's wonderful. When can she go home?"

"She can be discharged as soon as tomorrow, but she'll need a high level of care. She shouldn't be up and walking around for another week or two."

"I understand," she promised. "I'll stay with her."

After a few more instructions, the doctor started to walk away.

"Um, Doctor?" She felt weird asking him this, but she'd made two full circuits around the hospital and hadn't found what she needed. "Can you tell me where the restrooms are?"

He smiled kindly. "They're on the other side, near the elevators. But there's a smaller one down that hallway, third door on the right."

She made her way down the small offshoot hallway and came in sight of a large, thick window with no bars. It overlooked the city, in all its glory—or lack thereof. She could recognize many of the old buildings downtown and even the stadium of her high school, which was larger and taller than the school's building. The mostly flat skyline filled her with a sense of nostalgia for a simpler time and a smaller world. Now that she'd seen what lay beyond, she knew she'd never move back to this town.

Still, she felt gratitude for the mostly happy childhood it had given her.

A few chairs were lined up against the wall, and unlike those in the main waiting area, these were empty. She passed a utility closet stacked with white sheets and what appeared to be hospital gowns before finding the restroom.

After, she washed her hands and studied herself in the small mirror. No surprises there; she looked exhausted. She *felt* exhausted but also relieved. Her mother was well, even though there was her recovery to oversee. Blake was with her, even though they still needed to talk privately. Things weren't perfect. Even better, they were real.

As she stepped outside, she almost averted her gaze when she noticed someone else in the hallway. Then she paused.

"Blake?"

He turned at the sound of her voice. "What are you doing back here?"

He had been looking out the large window, his body drawn in lines of tension, leaning toward the window as if he could break free. His eyes were clouded with something dark and unsettled.

She gestured vaguely. "The restroom. Are you okay?"

"Of course."

Tension shimmered in the air. He looked on edge, his eyes sharp with an emotion she couldn't name. "You know, with Doug. Nothing happened."

"I know that."

"I thought you might worry, since he drove

me here." He said all the right things, but she knew he wasn't okay. It felt like walking off a cliff, that moment in a cartoon when you hung over the earth, waiting to fall. Her chest tightened. She forced herself not to reach for him.

"I'm sorry I wasn't there."

"No. I'm not angry. I was just worried about you…"

His smile was dark with self-recrimination. "I was playing pool, if you were wondering."

"Pool?"

"At the Faculty Ball. We went down to the basement. There wasn't any cell coverage."

It sounded so simple, but she felt her unease move through her bones. He hadn't been interested in another woman. He hadn't been spending the past few weeks realizing he could do better than her. Of course not. He was too loyal for that, but it didn't change the facts.

She wasn't worthy of him. Too poor, too young. Too helpless that she couldn't even drive home to her sick mother in a time of need. And he was a powerful man, probably drinking alcohol in some dimly lit parlor, talking about politics and knowledge.

"Do you want to go back to the waiting room?" she said, feeling almost shy.

"You go. I'll be there in a minute."

"Okay," she said, but she didn't move. Couldn't move. She had a memory of watching him stare out the window, of feeling his inner turmoil well in the air around him.

Only this was worse. More acute. Something was very wrong.

"Blake, you must be tired after that drive. Go back to the apartment and sleep."

He shook his head. "No, I'm fine. I want to be here for you."

Though he must be tired, she doubted that was the real problem. She stepped closer, noticing the light sheen of sweat on his forehead. The stubble on his jaw simply made him more handsome, but the shadows under his eyes gave him a vaguely haunted look.

"What's wrong?" she whispered.

He waved dismissively. "It's nothing. Just…hospitals. They have this effect on me. I'll get over it in a minute. You can go in to your mother. I'll join you soon."

Her heart sank. He must have had horrible memories from hospitals.

Once, very briefly, he'd explained some of the treatment he'd gone through after the explosion. The skin grafts and reconstruction. Weeks in an enemy torture chamber and then months under a doctor's scalpel. God.

Grief squeezed her lungs. "I'm so sorry. I didn't think."

"It doesn't matter. I'm sorry you even had to see me like this. That's why I came out here. It doesn't mean anything. It will be over soon."

"You shouldn't have to go through it alone," she said softly. She couldn't take away his waking nightmares, but she could hold his hand.

Turning away, he muttered, "Go."

"I can't do that."

Taking his hand, she led him into the small linen closet and shut the door.

"We shouldn't be here," he said as he leaned against the wall.

Clearly he'd been holding it together for her sake, and for the sake of anyone watching. Even she felt relieved to see him relaxed, so she could only imagine his discomfort. Easing him, even for a moment, was well worth the risk of discovery.

He stared at her through lowered lids. "What now?"

The challenge in his voice raised her chin.

He wanted to push her away, she could tell, but he wouldn't. He was incapable of leaving her any more than she could leave him. She brushed his lips with hers, enjoying the way he released a pent-up breath. The way she absorbed even small fractions of his stress into her body, giving him relief, easing him in the only way she could.

She feathered light kisses from one corner of his mouth to the other before he caught her bottom lip between his teeth. He tugged her, tilting her off balance. She fell into him, but he was prepared; he caught her. He slipped his tongue into her mouth and took over the kiss, deepening it, alighting her with dormant arousal.

The thickness against her belly reminded her that it had been weeks since they'd made love. They would have today, if this hadn't happened. No doubt they would have been ensconced in his bedroom, lounging on his bed, starving but with no desire to make the trek downstairs for food.

She put her hand to the ridge in his jeans, rubbing firmly. He sucked in a breath.

"What are you doing?"

She smiled against his mouth. "Giving you a new memory in a hospital."

With long, even strokes, she worked him through the denim. A slight flush of arousal crept up his neck. Between the time apart and his emotional upheaval a few minutes ago, he was already at the edge, releasing soft grunts on every slide of her palm.

She squeezed softly, enjoying the way his eyes had gone from tormented to a very different sort of anguish. Her hand sped up until he was panting against her collarbone, his hips rocking gently into her hand.

"Erin, baby. You have to stop."

"I know. You're right."

She dropped her to her knees and unzipped his jeans. His cock fell out heavy, the head already glistening.

"Please."

"I know," she repeated in a whisper. She took him into her mouth, sucking off the pre-cum and licking it up. She paused with her mouth encircling the head while her hand stroked the iron-velvet length of him. His stuttered groans drifted down to her ears, telling her how hard and fast he needed it. *Very* hard and fast.

Carefully, she worked him in deeper until the spongy head touched the soft cleft of her throat. She eased him out and then in again—farther in until the head pushed through the circle of muscles. His hips jerked suddenly and she gagged slightly. Before he could pull away or reconsider, she set up a swift pace—but she needn't have worried. He tightened his fingers in her hair, asking for more, needing it.

His other hand was clenched tightly, his knuckles white. She reached for him. As soon as her fingers touched his, he opened his fist and held her hand. Their fingers tangled together, grasped each other, connected in a way more intimate than her mouth on his cock.

"Erin."

That was the only warning he could manage before he shot warm, salty fluid into her waiting mouth. She swallowed down the copious amount, more than usual. With a shudder, he released one final spurt onto her tongue before sighing back against the wall. Lovingly, she licked up any traces of his cum from his cock before righting his clothes.

Her eyelids felt heavy, her sex throbbing for attention, but she wouldn't ask for anything, wouldn't expect it. This had been a gift.

She'd never understood the way some people could say "just sex" as if it didn't mean anything—sex had always meant everything. It meant trust and respect. Here, now, it meant love. If anything, it was too much, overflowing with emotion until she had to avert her face just to manage.

He turned her chin toward him. "I didn't hurt

you, did I?"

She shook her head tightly.

For a moment, he was still. She felt his gaze studying her, but she couldn't have said anything. Finally he straightened and turned her so her back was against the wall still warm from his body. Without a word, he unbuttoned her jeans and tugged them down.

"Blake," she protested. "We couldn't."

He raised a sardonic brow but didn't reply. Of course, they had just done the opposite. Her objections seemed silly in that context, but she had done that out of comfort, both for him and for her. And besides, logistically it was far easier to perform on him than on her. But he had it covered. His hand slipped beneath the elastic band of her panties and down into her wet folds. She gasped at the contact and grabbed his wrist.

His other hand lifted the hem of her T-shirt and tugged down the cup of her bra. Cool air washed over her breasts, tightening the nipple. For a moment, he simply stared.

"Gorgeous," he murmured, and she felt gorgeous. It was more than the word; it was in his expression and his hands. She felt worshipped. Cherished.

He sucked her nipple into his mouth, worrying the taut flesh with his tongue until she felt a gush of wetness slicken her where his fingers played. He teased her other breast while his fingers found a quick and maddening rhythm. Her mouth fell open and a sharp cry escaped her.

"Shh." He put his hand over her mouth, muffling her helpless sounds while he drove her higher and harder.

Her hips swiveled onto his hand in a desperate bid for release. It eluded her, until she sobbed against his mouth. From the corner of her vision, she could see her breasts move as her hips undulated. They drew him, his gaze, his mouth. He couldn't stop touching her and licking her. She couldn't stop rocking in excruciating pleasure. They were locked in shadows of arousal and agony, one bleeding into the other and then back again.

Finally he tore himself away from her breasts. He placed his lips above her ear, murmuring words of sex and longing. *You're so beautiful. So sexy. So wet all over my hand. I can feel how hot you are there, how tight, can you? Do you wish it was my cock inside you, filling you up? I do.*

Her cries grew louder, and his hand clamped down tighter. Tears of need slipped from the corners of her eyes until he found the words to push her over. *This sweet cunt, pretty cunt. It's mine. This and all of you. You know that, don't you? Now come for me. Let me feel this hot little cunt come all over me.* And it did, her muscles clamping down hard as an explosive climax swept through her and left her breathless and wrung out.

As she slowly returned to earth, he pressed light kisses across her mouth, mirroring the comfort she'd given him. With short strokes, he calmed the quaking, shivery muscles of her sex.

"There," he murmured. "You're okay. I've got you."

She marveled at how easily he had turned the tides. How quickly he had turned his own reward into hers. She'd wanted to bring him comfort, but his happiness was too tied up in her own, tightly woven threads she never wanted to unravel.

When he pulled away from her, he licked her juices off his fingers. She stared in hopeless fascination. Tilting her head back, he kissed her deeply, pushing her own musky flavor onto her tongue and, she knew, tasting the salt of his own release.

CHAPTER EIGHT

BLAKE

BLAKE CARRIED OUT the two bags of heart-healthy meals from the grocery store.

A small complication had kept Sofia Rodriguez in the hospital for two more days than the doctor had predicted. Erin had refused to leave except for brief showers, driving herself to exhaustion with the few hours of sleep she caught in the waiting area—but no amount of persuading convinced her otherwise. Erin was too loyal to do anything else.

He felt relief that both of them were in Sofia's home, sleeping.

Erin had given him a list of low cholesterol meats and whole grains to replace the cheap noodle packs and high-sodium soups currently stocking the kitchen. With little money and even less time to cook, Erin's mother had a pantry full of high-sodium foods. That had to change now, and it would, especially with Erin there to cook for the next couple of weeks.

They hadn't discussed beyond that yet.

Had she ever planned to return to Tanglewood permanently? If so, no wonder she'd been uncertain when he'd asked her to move in with him. She might have planned to move into this ramshackle apartment with her mother, to get a job in this small town.

What if she still wanted that?

He let himself into the back door using the key Erin gave him.

The upstairs was still quiet, so he set about putting the food away. Despite the dinner hour, he suspected the two women would sleep through the night, which would probably do them more good than a bite of food. He himself was bone tired and chugged down a glass of water before climbing the stairs.

He took a pit stop for a hot shower in the hallway bathroom, dressing in a fresh T-shirt and sweatpants he'd packed in a backpack shortly after hearing her voicemails.

He already knew which was the master bedroom from when he'd gotten Sofia's clothes while she was still in the hospital. And he knew which room was Erin's. The door was closed. That was probably a sign that he wasn't allowed inside.

They hadn't discussed where he would sleep. There wasn't a guest room, but there was a couch in the living room.

A gentleman would take the couch.

Blake wasn't a gentleman. Maybe he had been, once. That had changed when the IED blasted away half his face. He became something different, more animal. And he had been kept away from his mate for too long.

He opened the door.

Erin was sprawled on the bed, naked. God. Almost naked. Above the hem of the sheet, he could see the beige tone of her panties. Her breasts were small and pink-tipped in the dim light. Her jeans and T-shirt lay in a pile beside the bed. His chest swelled with tenderness. She must have dropped into bed, too tired even to change into pajamas.

Stripping down to his boxers, he climbed in behind her.

Her hair fanned across her pillow, reflecting the dim light like a still lake at midnight. Her even breathing was too quiet to hear—and yet he felt each soft exhale in his soul. Pale lashes fluttered against her cheeks as she dreamt. She was, in all ways, the epitome of peace. The opposite of him in every way. A balm to his battered soul.

When he'd first met her, he'd been sure he never deserved contentedness. He was too broken, too shameful, too horrified by what had been done to him and what he'd done in return.

On the day before they'd been rescued, Joe had stopped responding to external stimuli completely. Blake had kept his hand on Joe's wrist, feeling the weak pulse and waiting for them both to die.

When the SEAL team had shown up, mayhem had ensued. A saner man would have laid low until they had neutralized the threat. But Blake was out of his mind with grief and pain. He'd gotten hold of a gun and shot as many of his captors as he could find, until an American soldier had disarmed him.

How could he come back from that? He couldn't.

Survival. That's all he had ahead of him. Nights filled with pain from skin he no longer had. It burned again and again, despite the grafts and the medicine. Despite the months.

He'd never planned to recover, but the damned doctors were persistent. They'd pounded away with their surgical meat tenderizers until his body was functional again, but it had taken Erin to revive his heart. She'd done more than that, she'd become his heart.

Wherever she went, whatever she felt.

It was lovely and excruciating.

The delicate base of her neck peeked from her outswept hair.

The line of her spine was sinuous as her body twisted in sleep. Shadows pooled at the base of her back where the sheet ruched against her skin. His fingers twitched to trace the soft muscles and gentle lines, but he didn't want to wake her.

She stirred anyway, moving restlessly. Her face turned toward him, eyes still shut. He tried to soothe her before she came fully awake.

"I'm here. Just sleep."

As her body turned over, soft breasts pressed against his arm and drew his low groan into the air. His body responded, cock thickening, heart pounding. He felt the same carnal urge to claim, to mate, to please her. But above that sang a new melody, one he recognized as ancient—the desire to care for her. To nourish her, body and soul. That secret wish had imbued his actions at the grocery store, feeding her. And now as he ignored the demands of his body to let her sleep. Small gestures for feelings that ran impossibly, unendingly deep.

She flung her leg over him. Her calf touched his erection, the throb of selfish male flesh, and she stilled, coming awake enough to realize his condition.

"Never mind," he murmured. "We won't do anything. Just rest."

She didn't, though.

Half asleep, she fumbled beneath the sheet until she grasped his cock in her small palm. He made a coarse sound, his whole body stiffening. Her eyes remained closed as her soft, clumsy caresses drove him insane. He wasn't even sure she was totally awake, even when she slipped her panties off beneath the sheet.

He was two seconds away from pushing her away when she slid over him and centered her core above him. His mouth went dry as he stared at her breasts swaying slightly with her motion. Her nipples were dark brown and puckered with arousal, or the cold.

"Erin? Are you sure?"

The sound she made was muffled and indistinct, but it told him what he needed to know. *Shh,* it said. *I know what I'm doing. Let me take what I need.* He was, would always be helpless to refuse her. His arms fell to his sides, trembling with the effort not to hold her, touch her, make

SKYE WARREN

her move. He wanted to clasp her hips and force her down.

By tiny degrees, she slid around his cock.

The heat of her felt electric, sending shocks of pleasure through his balls and up his spine. He gritted his teeth and resolved not to come. She was exhausted, wrung out emotionally and physically. She needed comfort, not the rough, greedy fuck his body required.

Her eyelids still fluttered softly, lashes brushing her flushed cheeks.

She draped her body over him, pressing her breasts against his chest.

He allowed his hands to hold her then, to stroke her sides in uneven, soothing gestures—though it was really him being calmed, a backward caress. Her hips rolled, setting up a sleepy rhythm that had him ready to shoot in three subtle strokes.

Heat raced down his spine. The need to come felt like pinpricks all over his skin, but no, he wouldn't. Not while she needed him—not yet, not yet, not yet.

She nestled her nose under his chin, resting her face against his neck. Despite the torrent of sensation in his cock, he felt her breath against his skin. He rocked his hips up to her, meeting her on every stroke. Better than anyone, he knew about the bone-deep relief that could accompany sexual release. He would give that to her, even if it killed him.

Use me, he thought. *Take me. Fuck me.*

He forced himself silent, and she was quiet, focused. The only sound was skin pushing together, her cunt sucking him in and the insides of her thighs over his hips. He couldn't see straight, could no longer think with the intensity of her sex surrounding him, her slight weight blanketing him. He was lost in a haze, a fog of pure bliss.

Her orgasm clamped down on his cock.

Her hips jerked to a stop, shuddering on a final, lingering thrust. He didn't have the fast friction he needed to come, so his cock remained hard and throbbing within her. She stopped moving and made a contented sigh against the side of his neck.

He realized she had drifted off to sleep again.

With him still intensely aroused.

Tense, and drowning, he could still feel the velvety walls of her around his cock. Just thinking about her made his cock flex. But she was completely still over him, her breathing steady and slow. Gingerly, he moved her just enough to slip his cock from her slick heat, wincing at the cool sandpaper sheets on his sensitive flesh.

She was sleeping, and he wouldn't wake her, wouldn't fuck her, wouldn't give himself relief even if the alternative felt like pinpricks on his aching cock.

Gently he settled her against his side, and she nuzzled against his chest with a contented sigh. He swallowed, forcing back his desire and failing. It was going to be a long night with his cock throbbing with nowhere to go.

With one arm he cradled her close. With the other he reached for his phone. Maybe reading some of the doctorate theses would help him sleep. Even though he was interested in them, there was no denying the language was usually dry.

He tapped the email Jeremy sent him.

There were plenty of options, but he couldn't stop himself from opening Erin's thesis. He was so fucking proud of her. He almost wanted to wake her up and have her read it to him, but he wasn't that much of an asshole. So he scrolled down, enthralled, captivated, until he got to the part about a senator for upstate, and it felt like a punch to the gut.

ERIN

ERIN WOKE UP with a long, lazy stretch, hearing the gentle clink of pans and dishes in the kitchen. Rumpled sheets twined around her ankles, leaving a bare expanse of bed beside her.

Which meant Blake was out there with her mother.

A jolt of alarm went through her. What would they talk about? Would they get along? Blake was the most competent, charismatic man she'd ever met. She suspected he could charm a bird out of a tree if he put his mind to it, or in this case, charm a wary, protective mother into giving her blessings. But it was too important for her to relax.

Throwing on jeans and a T-shirt, she stumbled into the kitchen to find Blake standing at the stove and her mother chatting away with a conspiratorial smile.

Oh yes, the overprotective bird had most definitely left the tree.

"Telling all my secrets, hmm?" Erin asked, sitting at a place that had been laid out with a chipped plate and glass of orange juice.

"Of course not," her mother denied, the barely suppressed amusement belying her words. "Just that time in fifth grade when you had discovered

Robin Hood."

Erin groaned. "Oh God. That's even worse than I expected."

"What? It's cute."

A smile played at her mother's lips. It was good to see her enjoying herself, even if it was at Erin's expense. "Can we just show him pictures of me as a baby instead? That would be less embarrassing."

"You were adorable with your hair pulled up into that felt green hat. Those neighborhood boys didn't know what to make of you. You should have seen them staring."

"That is not a compliment, Mom." She sneaked a glance at Blake, who watched the byplay with undisguised amusement.

"I heard there was a bow and arrow," he added, his voice teasing.

Her mother sighed with pleasure. "The arrows had glittered feathers glued on."

"Okay, look," Erin said, finally rising to her own defense. "They were taking money out of the community center's donation box. It's not right. You can't fault my motives."

"I wouldn't dare," Blake said solemnly. "Not with you armed and dangerous."

She narrowed her eyes, promising retribution

when her mother wasn't in the room, but the effect was ruined by her grin. Oh well, it had been funny. Not at the time, when she'd been sure that injustice could be cured with a curved stick and some twine.

And somehow, it had worked, because like her mother had said, the boys had been too freaked out by her Robin Hood routine to really argue the point. They'd never touched the donations box again. Though she'd learned later in life that good intentions and bravery and a green felt hat weren't enough to right every wrong.

The thought stopped her cold. When had she become so jaded? During high school, with Doug? She wasn't sure, but none of that was true. Good intentions and bravery *were* enough. Maybe that was what had drawn her to Blake. He embodied both ideals.

Not even fire could stop him; his scars were testament to that.

He seemed to recognize the change in her mood, because he sobered. The playful light in his eyes gave way to a studied concern. Without taking her eyes off Blake, she spoke to her mother, who was sipping the last dregs of her coffee.

"If you're done here, I can set you up on the couch. You can watch some TV."

Her mother huffed. "I don't need help to make it to the living room."

"All the same, I'll walk you there."

She set her mother up with pillows and a glass of water too. Even with the doctor's blessing, she worried for her mother. And despite the urgency to return to Tanglewood, to pick up her relationship with Blake, she would stay until her mother would be fine on her own.

Sophie leaned on her arm as she stood from the table and crossed the short distance, proving that Erin was needed here for the time being. She found a blanket for her mother's feet and also a few beloved books for her to look at. She told herself she was just taking care of her mother, but at least partly, she was distracting her.

A burning, aching need had formed inside her—to talk to Blake, to hold him, and she couldn't very well do that with her mother looking on in the small space.

The television roared with laughter and voices as a morning talk show flickered on and captured her mother's attention. Erin bustled back into the kitchen under the pretense of cleaning up to find that Blake had already done so. He cooked, he cleaned. For her sick mother.

God, if she weren't already in love with

him…but she was.

Completely, hopelessly in love.

He glanced up from the sink of soapy water. "Why are you smiling?"

She went to stand behind him, wrapping her arms around his lean waist and resting her head against his back. "Just imagining doing this in your house when I get back. In our house."

He tensed in her arms, his muscles locking. "Erin."

She laughed at the note of warning in his voice. It was a sensual threat, the way his body readied for hers. "Unless you've changed your mind about me moving in with you."

"Does that mean you're going to move in with me?"

"It will probably be a couple of weeks until I can come back. I want to stay and make sure my mom is okay. But then… yes. If you still want me."

He turned around and pulled her in for a hug. His hands were wet and slippery on her arms, her hair, and she didn't care. "If I still want you. As if I could stop."

She nuzzled her face into his hard chest. "It's been forever."

"Forever and a day," he agreed, his voice

hoarse.

"When will you drive back?"

"To Tanglewood? I'm staying here with you."

"Of course not. You need to go back and prep for the fall semester."

"How did you know I was accepting the job?"

"Well, I wasn't sure," she admitted. "But I am now."

He huffed a laugh. "Very nice, my little socialist."

She groaned, remembering the Robin Hood story. Of course he would latch onto that. "You're going to actually call me that from now on, aren't you?"

"Absolutely. And I might need to see a costume. With tights."

"Fine, but you're playing Maid Marian."

"As long as you ravish me, I'll wear anything you want."

She laughed. He probably would wear anything she wanted him to. His masculinity could hardly be threatened when he stood there, so strong and solid, smelling of soap and a faint musk she could recognize in her sleep. And *had* recognized in her sleep, she realized, thinking of last night. A blush stole up her cheeks, remembering the feel of him.

His gaze honed on the color, and he bent to nuzzle against her neck. "Were you serious? You're coming to stay with me? Forever, Erin. I won't let you go after this."

"I couldn't joke about that," she said honestly. It meant too much. She *felt* too much. And she'd resigned herself to the fact that it wouldn't change anytime soon. Love had turned her into a raw, exposed nerve, and the only choice left was to seek the shelter of his embrace.

Tension ran through him, though he was silent. For a long moment, he said nothing, pressing light kisses down her neck and across her shoulder. "I'm grateful," he said thickly, and she knew she wasn't the only one who needed shelter.

She wrapped her arms around him, barely spanning him at all, but she felt him shudder. Her eyes half-closed, she blindly sought his mouth, finding it warm and firm against hers. She was in a daze, but he guided her, commanded her, until she found the sweet rhythm of their kiss and knew herself to be home—with him, holding him and being held.

"Go back to Tanglewood," she whispered. "Wait for me."

"Forever," he murmured. "You understand that I wouldn't stop. I'd wait for you forever.

Though if you came back sooner, I'd make it worth your while."

She smiled before tugging him closer for another kiss.

Chapter Nine

Erin

Three weeks later

DESPITE THE NUMBER of times Erin had undressed in Blake's bedroom, it felt strange to do so without his solid, sexy presence. And really it had been months.

The draft from the air conditioning raised goosebumps on her skin.

The slim light from between the closed curtains painted yellow light across her bare skin as she shucked her skirt and top. She paused with her thumbs tucked into her panties.

Was she really going to do this?

For all she knew, she'd look ridiculous splayed out on the bed. Blake hadn't, but then his body was hard, masculine, and completely unyielding. Hers, she admitted ruefully, was soft. He seemed to like her curves, but that didn't mean she needed to display them.

No, what was she thinking?

He was far more on display every single day—to strangers, no less. And on that unlikely afternoon when she had caught him masturbating, he had exposed himself to her. His pleasure, his body. His heart. It was only fair she return the favor.

She toed off her panties and unhooked her bra, letting it fall to the floor amid the other puddles of clothing. Half-bending, she almost picked them up to fold them…stalling, of course. Even determined, the urge to delay, to hide, tugged at her.

No more waiting. Blake could pull up at the house any minute.

She couldn't reproduce the element of surprise, considering her repaired car was out front. But she could make the vulnerability real. The moment of unvarnished intimacy.

Climbing onto his bed, she settled herself back, feeling unaccountably raw. Her nipples pebbled in the chilly air even while her face heated with embarrassment. When she slipped trembling fingers down to her sex, she found her lips dry and curled up tight.

She closed her eyes and swallowed hard. This required a little imagination.

What had he been thinking of that day?

She remembered now. Her mouth, his cock. She'd sucked him in that little fantasy, and goddamn, it worked for her too. She loved the taste of him, the shape of him, the little ridge underneath, perfect for hooking her tongue around and making him shudder. Imagining it now, she touched two fingers lightly to her clit, warming herself up through contact alone.

No pressure, no friction—just a whisper touch.

Letting her mind drift, she fell deeper into the fantasy.

The hair on his thighs abraded the sensitive outer curve of her breasts as she knelt between his legs. His hands shifted restlessly through her hair, clenching and releasing as if he couldn't decide which to do. He groaned on every stroke of her lips down his slippery cock. His whole body drew up tight when she angled the point of her tongue into the slit, and she could almost taste the salty pre-cum.

She imagined him finding her. Would he be surprised? Or maybe not. The things they had done were far dirtier than fondling her clit or pinching her own nipples. And yet, a shaky feeling had begun in her center, warning her, berating her. *Don't put yourself out there,* it said.

Wait. Just wait. For what, though? She'd never quite understood. For the man to make the first move. For her mother to direct her safely through life.

For Blake to decide she was strong enough to stay.

Well, screw that. Her relationship with Blake may have started awkwardly, and mortifyingly, but she had always been an equal participant. Her mother may have raised her, but these past few weeks, Erin had taken care of her.

And she hoped Blake didn't doubt her anymore, she truly did.

But the important thing was that *she* knew she was strong enough to stand beside him, whatever problems he might face. His physical injuries, which still pained him. The PTSD which probably always would. And the incipient self-doubt that would always lurk in the shadows of this powerful, confident male. She could handle any of it, all of it. She *had* done so for their entire time together, and she'd never been happier than she was with him.

She knew, without ego or artifice, that he was happiest with her as well.

Love wasn't a lightning strike, a sharp point with a definite beginning and an inevitable end. It wasn't a flash that was over before you could even register the pain. Love was a shelter from the storm, respite from her fears and relief from the reality of his scars.

The air around her shifted, but instead of cold, her skin grew warm.

Little sparks on her nipples and aiming down to her core let her know she was being watched. The sense of contentedness that entered her body let her know who it was. Her sex grew slicker under the regard, but she kept her eyes firmly shut.

This was for him...and for her. A wintry undercurrent of shame made her arousal burn hotter. Soft footfalls on the carpet drew closer.

A gentle caress touched her lips. "Beautiful," he said.

Above all, she knew him to be honest, and the fact that he found her beautiful, the fact that he found her mouth or face beautiful when her whole body was exposed to him, made her heart clench. A tear leaked from her closed eyelid.

He caught it with his finger and traced its path back up her cheek.

"Don't be sad," he said, and she heard the sadness in his voice—an ineffable sorrow for what he had seen, for what he had been through. If there was anyone who understood suffering, it was him. And yet, he seemed to derive more joy than anyone she knew.

He found it in her body, in her company. He found it in books and teaching. He found joy in living again, and her love for him was boundless, expanding.

"Oh, Blake," she said, too choked up to say anymore. Her tears fell in earnest then.

He released himself; at least, that was how it felt to her. He scooped her up and cradled her. She didn't fail to notice the nudge of his arousal, but he wouldn't use it until he knew she was okay. She *was* okay. Better than okay, which spilled over into sadness and then back again in an eternity knot of powerful, life-affirming emotions.

One couldn't be separated from the other.

She couldn't have known love without heartache.

He couldn't have found solace without pain.

"Don't cry," he murmured against her hair. "What was this about? To show me that you want me, that you care. I know that, sweet girl. Don't you think I know that? You show your heart in every expression, and it's beautiful to see."

Somehow she found her voice. "You can't talk like that and expect me not to cry."

His chest expanded on a quiet laugh. "There's my girl."

She turned her face into his chest, her cheeks wet and slippery against his shirt. Fumbling, she tugged it over his head, desperate to feel him, skin-to-skin, nothing between them. His body felt sharp after the long absence, the rigid planes of muscle, the hair tickling her tender skin. She shuddered against him, leaning closer, aching to feel him harder, more deeply. And thank God, he seemed to understand; he seemed to need it too, holding her flush against him, almost bruising her, needing her.

He turned them over, so she lay on her back, the sheets cool against her skin. His mouth held her down, his hands explored her, caressed her all over, and then he began to move down. Nipping kisses down her neck and in the valley of her breasts, gentle kisses over the curve and suckling at the tip. Then he trailed lower, as her belly quivered beneath questing lips.

"Blake," she said, in warning, in plea.

"Just take it," he murmured. "Be good for me," and she was lost and lax in his arms.

Her legs fell open, letting him explore the insides of her thighs.

He made a small sound of pleasure as he felt

the wetness at her core. Possessive fingers dipped into the moisture and spread it across her swollen flesh. He drew damp circles around her clit until any traces of reserve had fled. Spearing her, he pulled more of her arousal to the entrance. He removed his hand from her, and with damp fingertips, drew a heart on the low flat of her belly.

She smiled in her sensual haze and reached for him. He caught her hand in answer and sucked on the tip of her finger, sending shocks down her center. Then he ducked his head to lick up the mess he had made of her—her belly first, his tongue mapping the shape of the heart. Then lower, down to the outer lips, then inner. He roamed to her clit, which had grown too sensitive, and she jumped, startled, entranced.

"Please," she groaned, not sure what she was asking for. Relief or respite, more or less. It all blended together in a miasma of desire. "Blake."

"You can take it," he said, softer now, encouraging. He pushed her legs up, farther and more firmly than he usually did. Her knees pressed against her chest, capturing her, exposing her. His eyes burned with a hungry light as he stared down at her.

"Please," she repeated.

Keeping both hands on her thighs, he bent to place hot, open-mouthed kisses against her sex, sucking and licking until she squirmed. But he held her too tightly to move much or escape—and thank God, because she didn't want him to stop, not really.

She wanted more and harder. Her secret muscles clenched in silent question, begging to be filled, but empty as he teased her clit to oblivion.

"You're mine," he muttered, his breath a phantom caress against her sex. "I won't let you go now. There's no escape. Only this. Only my mouth on you. My cock inside you."

Yes. His. *"Please."*

He chuckled darkly. "You'll have to learn patience. Well, we'll have a lot of time to practice. A lot of time to play with this pretty little pussy. To make it wet and swollen."

Then he put his mouth to her clit and her whole world went black, with stars bursting behind her eyelids. Before she recovered he entered her, thrusting roughly, without rhythm or finesse, so perfect that tears slipped down her cheeks. She came two more times before he became rigid above her, still rocking as he poured himself inside her.

She accepted it all. His come, his sweat. His

love.

He leaned on her, breathing hard. She caught him when he wanted to roll off, mumbling something about being heavy. He *was* heavy, and perfect, and she wanted to feel that lovely weight forever. Enough to make her pant, to make her struggle. A beautiful fight.

"Marry me," she whispered.

He stiffened. After a moment, he pulled back, searching her eyes. "What did you say?"

She smiled. "You heard me, Professor."

"Did you...did you plan to ask me?"

"No." Other couples arranged champagne and fancy dinners. "But I think we should start the way we meant to go on. Or go on the way we started."

With sex. Masturbation, to be specific. But more than that.

With an attraction so deep they had to act on it. With respect so strong they'd been careful and mindful and *joyful* every step of the way. Unconventional, unique, or just freaking weird—she didn't care. This was the way their relationship had started, his moment of vulnerability a gift to her, and she'd wanted to propose to him and return the favor.

"Well, Professor?" Her heart started to beat

faster.

A slow smile spread over his face. "Erin."

Which wasn't an answer, really. She raised an eyebrow.

"God, you're beautiful." He reached over to the side table.

Still not an answer. "If you're going to grab a sex toy right now, I might have to rethink my proposal. There's only so much I can put myself out there."

But he didn't have a sex toy, judging by the little black box. If she'd thought her heart was beating fast before, it was nothing compared to now. He opened it to reveal a sparkling princess cut diamond with small, even diamonds circling the band. Her heart stopped.

The words came to her in a rush: *If you can paint...I can walk...* If he could move past his scars, return to the world, the very least she could do was move past her own fears and trust him not to leave. *The world can turn upside down...* And it did.

"Yes," he said simply. "I'll marry you."

He did more than answer her; he asked, with the ring that had been stowed away in his side table drawer...for how long? Happiness squeezed her throat, robbing her of breath. She had to force the words, to feign levity or she'd never be able to speak at all. "Now, I said no sex toys. But I have to tell you, that right there is very sexy."

His mouth curved in a self-satisfied little smile. "I think it'll look great on you. Wearing nothing else. This means that you belong to me. And that I belong to you."

"Oh, so this was all a ploy to get me naked," she said, clearly teasing since she was already naked and so was he. "Naked except for this."

"It seems to be working," he said, slipping the ring on her finger.

It sparkled in the dim evening shadows, reflective even with barely any light. But no glittering facets or sleek metals could compete with the stark, painful beauty of the man in front of her. The man she loved.

BLAKE

BLAKE LINGERED IN the hallway, watching Erin flip a page in the newspaper.

His body tightened at the sexy sight. Sun streamed in through the bay windows, glinting golden off her hair and illuminating the lines of her body within her white dress shirt. His dress shirt, although she still wore it much better than he ever would. The top buttons were undone, allowing him a glimpse of the curve of her breast as she bent her head, intent on her reading.

She glanced up and smiled. "Good morning."

"Morning." He wandered into the breakfast nook, feeling reluctant to disturb her. As if it were her room, her house. And God, it was. "You look beautiful today. And every day."

She'd agreed to marry him, which meant all this was hers as much as his. A sense of contentment filled him at the thought. He'd be able to take care of her.

And, he thought wryly, he'd be taken care of in return. She satisfied his every need. The taste of her, the sweet swell of her pussy against his lips. The tender kiss she gave his cock.

He didn't slow until he reached her, standing beside her chair, tilting her chin up to look at him. He brushed his thumb over her lips, loving the way she shivered in response.

"You're happy," he said. A statement, a question? He wasn't sure.

"Too much." She smiled shyly. Was she blushing? "I'm not sure what I did to deserve this. Or what you did this morning. My legs are still kind of shaky."

Jesus, she killed him. Humble and proud,

kind and fierce. A study of contradictions in a beautiful package he would never get tired of worshipping. Like a magnet, his lips sought hers; he bent to kiss her, leaving them both breathless.

Sometime during the onslaught, her hands grasped his bare shoulders. He was wearing only his dress pants from last night, picked up off the floor. It seemed they could only find a full set of clothes between them—and no underwear. No bra, that much he could see. Damn, he was going to have a hard time leaving her in peace today. And every day. Especially considering the ring that sparkled on her finger. His ring. The sight of it filled him with possession.

With peace.

"I'm not going to let you go now. You know that, don't you?" He didn't know why he was always warning her. Even now, he thought she might leave.

Why hadn't she told him about her thesis?

He knew the answer.

Because he had pushed her away, by making him take a break. He couldn't even fully regret that decision, not when her future was at risk. No, it was only their future as a couple at risk. Didn't she trust him? She agreed to become his wife. He'd thought that would sate him, but it seemed that nothing would be enough when it came to her.

She grinned. "Do you think I'd let you go either? Not a chance. So get comfortable, mister. You're going to be mine."

Ah hell. No way was he leaving her in peace today. He pulled her from the chair, flush against his body, molding his hands to her curves. "God, I already am."

He kissed her again, debating whether they could make it upstairs to the bedroom. But then she kissed him back—actually nipped his lower lip—and he stopped thinking at all. He surrounded her, body and heart; he sank into her, finding refuge in her sweet acceptance and limitless love.

There were no boundaries on what he would do for her. He would climb mountains, slay dragons—but all she'd ever asked of him was a promise. And so he had always been hers, before he'd even known it, stumbled upon in moment's base weakness, claimed by a whole-hearted acceptance, and made new by a love he would work to deserve each coming day.

He only vaguely remembered some hint of scandal while he'd been in basic training, but he'd assumed it was an affair. A consensual affair. His throat tightened imagining what could have happened to a young woman in a vulnerable position, what an unscrupulous employer might do. Proposition her? Touch her?

Hit her?

It made him sick that it could happen to anyone, but even more so because Erin had been in just as vulnerable a position when she'd cleaned his home. The thought of anyone harming her made him see red.

CHAPTER TEN

BLAKE

IT SOUNDED LIKE thunder and felt like an earthquake, vibrating right down to his bones.

Not anything natural like a storm, not with the smell of burnt air and fuel left behind. Two F-22 Raptors had swooped low to the ground, right overhead, their presence just a blur in his retina. He squinted through the leaves, waiting. Even the trees seemed to shudder, holding their breath. The blast came two miles to the south, on the other side of the low mountain range.

"What the fuck are they doing?" Ricardo's voice was strained, high-pitched. He had his hand on his helmet as if that would somehow keep it on, keep him safe.

Blake knew they were fucked, helmets or not. "We gotta get to the checkpoint."

But he wasn't about to tell his teammate the truth. It wouldn't help to panic. It wouldn't help to know they'd die anyway. The military had decided they were expendable. In that moment they were just as much the enemy as the terrorists hiding in a damn cave. Like the civilians here, the women and the children and the hard-working men, they were fucking collateral.

"We'll never make it," Ricardo said, panting.

No, they wouldn't. "We get to the checkpoint and we get out. We stick to the damn plan."

His teammate nodded—too fast, too frantic. "Okay. I can do that."

"I know you can," Blake said, low and fierce. Even young and green, Ricardo toed the line. Their entire team was a fucking powerhouse—or they had been until they'd been picked off one by one by snipers on the ridge.

The ridge should have been cleared and the birds should have waited until they were clear to strike, but none of that mattered now.

Ricardo's face twisted in grief, a thin wet track through the thick layer of dirt on his cheek. "I won't let them die for nothing."

Blake took the man by the back of the neck and pulled him in. Forehead to forehead. They were close. Teammates. Brothers. The last two fucking men on this godforsaken patch of earth. His chest seized tight. "No matter what, they didn't die for nothing," he said. "No matter what, it meant something. Now we're going to get to the goddamn checkpoint like they'd want us to do."

"Yeah." Ricardo's voice got stronger. "We're going to get out."

Blake wasn't so sure about that, but there was no better plan. No plan at all except the one that had already gone to hell.

They fought through thousands of feet of dense jungle, wary of an ambush at any moment. They ran over exposed flat rock, expecting a bullet from an unseen shooter to take them out all the way.

And somehow—an actual fucking miracle—they made it to the checkpoint.

"Empty," Ricardo breathed.

Empty. And the hollow feeling in Blake's stomach couldn't be surprise, could it? He'd known this would happen. He'd known as soon as the first man had fallen, that something had gone horribly wrong. They wouldn't make it out of this.

He wasn't even sorry for himself. He had the strangest thought that his fiancée wouldn't mind if he never came back. His parents would milk the tragic hero story until they'd made it to the fucking White House. And his work? It was just a bunch of smoke and mirrors—the political stage, the historical backdrop. Intellectual sleight of hand to cover up *this*, the living and breathing, the fighting and dying of men that amounted to nothing.

No, he wasn't sorry for himself but he was seriously pissed about Ricardo. Ricardo had a brother. They'd lost so many men today but right now all he could think about was Ricardo's little brother. He idolized him—and wasn't Ricardo too young to be an idol? To be a fucking martyr?

He wasn't much younger than Blake, not in years, but a few tours made all the difference.

Then he heard it—the whoop of a chopper, so faint he might have imagined it.

"What the fuck," he breathed.

Ricardo looked wary. "You hear something?"

Not insurgents. He hoped not anyway. And there it was, the chopper come to take them away. Only a few minutes late. It was a miracle. A miracle kicking dust into their eyes. They ran to the side, giving the chopper room to land.

That was the only thing that saved them when the first bullet hit the ground.

Under fire. They were under siege.

Had the enemy been waiting for the chopper to land so they could take it?

For a second, the chopper hovered, and Blake was sure it would fly right up again, taking with it any chance of rescue or hope. *Ricardo's little brother.*

But then it battered almost gently against the hard-packed earth, landing only seconds before the door slid open. A barrel appeared, taking shots near the tree line, providing the cover he and Ricardo needed to make it inside.

"Let's go," Blake shouted over the heavy thrum of the propellers. He pushed Ricardo in front of him so he'd cover behind. They both ran.

They reached the door of the chopper. An arm came out to pull them inside.

Blake was already standing in the heavy vibrating machine when he looked back and saw Ricardo crumple to the ground—outside the chopper. "Get up," he shouted. He didn't care if it was cruel to drive him like this. They'd leave without him.

Their cover was gone.

"Move," the man shouted into his headset—telling the pilot to go.

Blake moved to jump out, but the man blocked him. The other man had fifty pounds on him, as well as more nights of sleep in the past 72 hours and more food and water. But Blake had the fucking determination, the certainty that he couldn't, wouldn't leave his teammate behind. His last one. The only man left. If there was anyone left behind on this rock, in this oven, it would be him.

A shot hit the chopper—impossible to know where. It rocked the whole machine, and Blake fell off balance. The doors were still open, but tilted up, and Blake was sliding back, falling. Every second took him farther from Ricardo, every second took him one more foot in the air.

"No," he roared, lunging for the doors. It would almost kill him to make the jump now, but he didn't care. This wasn't happening. This couldn't fucking be happening.

The guy caught him by the ankle just as he was almost out of the chopper.

He landed hard on the metal grate. The force of his fall swung the chopper far enough that he could see over the edge: the man sprawled on the ground, wounded. And he could see the other men, closing in now that the chopper was leaving range, surrounding him like a pack of wolves.

"No." This time it was only a quiet sound, stricken. Too soft to hear over the roar of the bird.

Ricardo's brother. *Ricardo.*

Something wasn't right. The bullet must have struck something vital, because the engine was sputtering now. They were still in the air but shifting sideways. At this height they'd crash. They'd burn.

And then they didn't have to wait that long. A flare of orange out of the corner of his eye was the only clue the chopper would explode in the split seconds before it did, before flames engulfed him, before the force of the blast threw him from the chopper, and then he was falling, falling out of the sky.

BLAKE

"GET UP!"

Blake jerked from sleep, breaths bellowing in and out of his chest, blood racing. His body was covered in sweat and tangled up, constrained, tied down by fabric and hands.

Something warm was beside him, something soft.

He grew still. His eyes closed. "I'm sorry. Did I wake you?"

Of course he'd woken her. He always woke her when he got like this.

In fact, she was the one who had to wake him

up, because he wouldn't stop thrashing and screaming. How many years had it been now? He'd come back, put his life together. He'd found Erin. Things were good, but the nightmares wouldn't stop. Would they ever?

Erin trembled beside him. He could feel her tremors through the mattress they shared. A strip of moonlight fell over her face. Her eyes were wide, lips tight. Fear. She was afraid of him.

His stomach clenched. "What did I do?"

She shook her head, her voice shaking only slightly when she said, "Nothing."

A lie. "What did I do to you?"

Her hands tightened and released a twisted corner of the sheet. "You were... on me."

Something inside him went cold. He didn't want to believe it. But maybe that was just a sign of how fucked up he was, that he wasn't even surprised. Angry. Furious. At himself. But not even fucking surprised. "I was hurting you?" he asked softly.

"No." The word came out too forcefully—too false. "Not on purpose. You were... I think you were protecting me. You kept saying to stay down."

"Jesus." He shook his head and looked at the wall. *Jesus.*

He was one fucked up soldier. What business did he have with a woman like her?

"Are you okay?" he asked. He didn't wait for her to answer. He ran his hands over her shoulders, her arms, assuring himself that she was put together, her body just as whole, her skin just as smooth. His dream self may have been trying to protect her, but he could have hurt her in the process. He was a brute, an animal, and she was so fragile.

"I'm fine," she said, and at least her voice did sound more normal now.

Maybe he'd just scared her more than hurt her, but either way it was too damn close. Even if he'd been in a dream, if he'd believed that somehow he was protecting her, he'd used his body to dominate her. He could have injured her and not even known it. Or God, what if his dream self had thought of her as the enemy? He could kill her.

Snap her pretty little neck before he was even awake.

Abruptly, he stood. The master bedroom was large, but suddenly it felt suffocating. He paced away from the bed, away from her, moving to stand at the window. So many nights he'd looked out of this window, awake again, panting and sweating again.

When would the nightmares stop?

He heard the sheets rustle as Erin got out of bed.

Her footsteps were soft over the hardwood floors. And then she was behind him, her arms around his waist, her lips pressed to his back. So many nights he'd stood here, staring out the window, and so many nights, she'd stood behind him, kissing him, making him whole again.

He knew she deserved better, deserved someone already whole, but he couldn't give her up. Not when it seemed almost bearable with her here.

After a few minutes of stroking his chest, of pressing light kisses to his back, she said, "Come back to bed."

He nodded. "Soon."

"Not soon," she said gently. "Now. We have to be up early tomorrow."

The plan was to drive to his parents' house tomorrow. It was a few hours away—and yet didn't feel nearly far enough. "I'll still be able to drive."

She made a sound of protest. "I know you will, but I want you to feel okay too. Come on. I'll help you relax."

His body stirred at just the suggestion. Hell, he was half-hard whenever she was around. Now was no exception. His cock already formed a tent in his boxers. It would only grow painful if she kept touching him, kept pressing those lovely breasts against his back, kept her warm breath against his skin.

His hips actually bucked, his body blindly seeking her, an animal instinct, a need.

He felt her lips curve in a smile. "I didn't mean that," she said. "But we could."

Except he didn't like to fuck her when he'd just woken up from one of the nightmares. It felt too dirty, like letting her get close to that moment and all the darkness that infected him. He also didn't quite trust himself right after one of those dreams, still shaky and overly alert.

Especially after he'd been fucking holding her down.

"Let me hold you," he said instead. He wanted to hold her gently, sweetly. He wanted to erase every rough touch he'd used on her a few minutes ago. He wanted to erase those memories she had of him doing that, but he knew well how impossible that would be.

Wordlessly she took his hand and led him back to bed.

After she climbed in, he curved his body around hers. God, she was warm and soft. It was like fucking heaven to feel her in his arms. It scared him sometimes, how good she felt. Like he might hold her too tight, might force her to stay even if she'd be better off gone.

He let out an uneven breath.

She stroked her fingers over the back of his hand, rhythmic and soothing. "You're okay. I've got you."

He pressed his face into her hair. She smelled so fucking good. His arms tightened around her. He forced himself to relax a fraction, to let her breathe. But not much, because he needed her. Needed to hold her, to feel her safe and whole with him.

There were questions he wanted to ask her. Like if he'd hurt her while he was dreaming. If he'd hurt her before tonight. He wanted to know if she was happy with him, truly. But he knew what her answers would be. She was fine, fine, fine. He wasn't sure she'd ever tell him if she wasn't.

She was too damn strong for her own good.

His heart had stopped racing, his nerves had cooled. She had that effect on him. His dick was also hard as a fucking flagpole. She had that effect on him too, especially with her ass pressed up against him.

He smoothed his hand over her hip and down between her legs. Soft. Wet. Fucking heaven.

A small hitch in her breath was the sound of her assent. That and the widening of her thighs, giving him more access. She always let him in, and at least in this one thing, he could give her pleasure. He could make her feel good.

As long as he kept the dark side of him in check.

As long as he kept the beast locked up.

ERIN

ERIN SHUDDERED AS his thick finger slid through her folds.

God, she was slick. She could hear the sounds of her wetness. Her cheeks burned with humiliation. It was one thing for a man to wake up hard. That was normal. Natural. But this?

Her body was constantly primed for him. As if it knew he might roll on top of her and slide inside at any moment—and he did. She'd wake up clenching around him, her hips already rocking. She didn't need to be awake for him to make her come.

He gave her the best dreams.

Her body was ready, but her mind was... worried. Worried about the dark expression on Blake's face, the loneliness in his stance. Sex distracted him, but it was a temporary fix. Then again, there was no permanent fix. Not to war. Not to the scars that covered his body. No permanent fix for the ones inside him.

"Wait," she gasped. "Let me..." She wasn't sure what she'd do. Stroke him. Tell him everything would be okay, even if it wouldn't. Something, anything.

He was already shaking his head. She felt the motion of it just like she felt his arm tighten around her, his fingers stroke more forcefully. His touch was merciless on her body.

"I want to make you feel good," he muttered against her neck, and she was helpless then. Helpless except to relax her legs completely as he stroked and stroked.

He was hard and big against the small of her back. His fingers weren't entering her. They just teased at the opening, taunting her. "Fuck me," she moaned. "Please."

"Yes," he muttered, sounding hard, unforgiving. His masterful fingers, his endless teasing was all the answer he would give. She bucked her hips mindlessly, trying to grasp those thick fingers, trying to fuck them. He wouldn't let her, always pulling away, bringing her to the brink only to push her back again. She was gasping, crying, begging.

Begging him, when she should have had more pride than that.

It physically hurt, how much she needed him. "Please, Blake. Fuck me."

Only then did he move. But it wasn't to mount her.

His shoulders were between her thighs, his head bent, before she could say no. She wanted his cock inside her, filling her up. Only then did she feel complete. Only then did she feel safe, knowing that he wasn't thinking of anything but this.

"Stop," she managed to say. Only that. *Stop*.

He looked up, his expression severe. "You don't want me to kiss that pretty pussy? You don't want me to suck your soft skin or lap that little clit? You don't want me to shove my tongue as far as I can inside you, feeling your inner muscles tighten?"

Her sex clenched at his words. She wanted all of that.

All of him, forever and always.

There was something forced and almost frantic about the way he held her, as if he thought she might disappear. That wasn't forever. And the way he'd sometimes go away, his eyes dark and opaque, the past almost a living thing in the room—that wasn't always.

His voice got low. Seductive. "You want me to push my tongue into your slit, fuck you with it? Then I'll shove two fingers inside—no, three. That's all it'll take to hold you still, three fingers inside you. You'll be so full of me, you won't be able to move. I wouldn't have to hold down your hips or your hands, but you still wouldn't be able to move. Pinned down by three fingers in your pussy. You'd fuck herself on my hand. You wouldn't be able to stop."

Her breathing grew heavy. "Blake."

"That's right, baby," he said, and the approving note in his voice made her rock against him, seeking his lips, his tongue. His three fingers. "And while I'm holding you still like that, from the inside out, that's when I'll suck on your clit."

She pressed her heels into the bed, pushing up, begging with her body. All she succeeded in doing was brushing her sex against his chin, and the bristles there made her ache in the best ways. "It hurts inside," she whispered. "Hurts because you're not there."

He chuckled. "Impatient."

"Always," she gasped.

"Then you aren't going to like this." He bent his head and finally, finally dragged a long slow lick from the bottom to the top of her slit, each millimeter as long as a mile, while she writhed and moaned. "I'm going to take a long time with you tonight. I'm going to spend a long time tasting this pretty pussy, drawing out every drop of that sweet come. I won't stop until you're begging me. I won't stop until you're crying because you need it that bad."

"I'm begging you now," she moaned.

He pressed a quick kiss to her mound. "Not yet."

Not enough. "Please."

His expression was tender but his voice was stern. "Hands above your head, sweetheart. Hold onto your pillow. Don't let go of it. Whatever you do, don't let go."

"Oh God." She reached up and did as instructed, grasping the sides of the pillow.

Already her body was thrashing against her will, as if she could climb him, as if she could climb the peak—but she couldn't. He wouldn't let her until he was good and ready.

If there was one thing the man had most of all, it was patience. He drew out their lovemaking to last hours. They were both sweaty and exhausted by the time he was done. And most of all, incredibly sated. She longed for those nights as much as she feared them. They were more than a sexual act, they were a test, and sometimes it felt like they would break her.

He nibbled at her pussy with his lips and with light touches of his teeth that made her squirm. He spread her wide with his fingers and feasted, leaving no part of her untouched. He bathed her with his tongue until she could only clench and clench at nothing, could only keen in helpless unfulfilled desire.

It might have been minutes or hours or days that he played with her, tasting her and teasing her. Barely brushing her clit and then roaming back down to her slit. He fucked her entrance with his tongue like it was a cock, and it felt somehow sweeter than his cock—but less fulfilling too. She'd never come this way, never come at all, she'd be forever strung up on his tongue and fingers and relentless, bittersweet patience.

Only when she'd come again and again, when her body was wrung out, somehow tighter and more needful after climaxing three times, did he raise his head. She panted on the bed, clinging to the pillow, fabric clenched and sweat-damped in her hands.

"Take me," she said, her voice soft and broken.

Tears streamed down her cheeks. He'd done that to her. Just like he promised he would.

He pushed up, onto his knees, and for one heartbreaking minute she thought he would leave her like this. His eyes flickered with that distance, that darkness—the same one he had after every one of his nightmares. His broad chest expanded, and his breath came out in a harsh groan of giving in.

He was on her a second later, firm hips pressing her thighs open, chest looming over her, expression hard. His hands were on either side of her shoulders. He didn't touch himself, didn't guide himself inside. There was no need for that, not when their bodies fit together like sea and sky, like light and dark. His cock nudged her entrance and slid inside, stretching her walls, filling her up and making her clench down around him.

She gasped out a wordless thanks, gratitude and desire all tangled up in the physical sensation. Even with how long he had licked her, how swollen and ready she was for him, it still felt like a stretch for him to slide all the way inside. A memory made real.

He bent his head. A whisper in her ear, hoarse and hungry, "Come for me. One more time, beautiful. I need to feel it around my cock. I need that hot liquid all around me and trickling down my balls. Can you do that for me?"

But he didn't need to ask the question; she was already coming, already squeezing him tight and bathing him in her wetness. And then he was coming too, pushing back against her with heavy pulses of his cock and thick spurts of come deep inside.

CHAPTER ELEVEN

ERIN

"**E**RIN?"

She blinked once, twice, and the book came into view. It was large, with that old library smell she loved to breathe in. Even though she liked the smell of the book, she couldn't say the same for its contents. They hadn't managed to keep her awake—and she'd been reading out loud.

"Sorry," she said, feeling sheepish. Bad enough that she would doze off while reading a book. Much worse to have been caught by Blake, who had read The Philosophy of History multiple times.

"I'm the one who should feel bad for boring you. I picked the book."

"That's only fair. I got to pick the last one." Her choice had been the diary of novelist and eroticist Anais Nin. He'd read it to her while she'd attempted to bake homemade bread. It had turned them both on so much—explicit words in his deep voice, her hands plunging into soft dough—that they'd made love on the kitchen floor until the bread had burned.

So when they'd loaded the car for their trip, she'd offered to read him his choice while he drove.

He smiled faintly, his hands steady on the steering wheel. "Fair or not, I'm more than happy to have you pick our books from now on. I'll save the Hegel and the Kant for my students."

"Kant? I'm thinking you're a bit of a sadist."

"Only with books. And only in the classroom. When it's just you and me, I only want to make you feel good."

Her cheeks flushed, and judging by the amused expression on his face, he knew it too. If only there was a kitchen floor nearby. Unfortunately they were far away from Blake's ranch-style home, with its seclusion and comfort. With every mile they drove, her stomach had tightened another notch. She'd hoped reading would distract her, but it had only put her to sleep.

Blake reached over and took the book from her lap. He put it in the backseat without taking his eyes off the road. Her gaze followed the lines of his muscular arms, his torso as it was exposed to her. How did he make even ordinary actions so sexy? She would catch him stroking the spine of a book or reaching for something on a high shelf, and her body would heat up.

"You should sleep," he said gently. "We have another hour to go."

"Are you sure you don't want to trade off?"

"I'm sure. Go ahead and rest."

"I'm not sure I can," she admitted.

He glanced over, concern darkening his expression. She hadn't said anything particularly revealing, but maybe he'd heard the tremor in her voice. "What's wrong?"

She shook her head. "Nothing."

"Erin. Baby."

That was all it took to twist her up. Him saying her name. Him calling her the sweet endearment, the one he used when they were tangled up in bed together, so tight and twisted she wasn't sure they could ever break apart—and she wouldn't want them to. But this trip, this felt like breaking apart. His home was their cocoon, where their relationship had begun, where they'd fallen in lust and in love.

Of course they'd have to leave it sometime. They were engaged now. If anything, it was late in their relationship to be meeting his parents for the first time.

"I'm a little nervous," she said on a soft breath.

"Ah, baby. I understand that. I do. But I'm going to be by your side the entire time."

"I know," she said, although she didn't really. His parents came from old money. Heck, Blake came from money. And that was a foreign world to her. A scary one.

He cleared his throat. "Are you worried about it because of your mom?"

She didn't flinch. Didn't do anything that would give away how even the thought of her mother made her feel. It would only make Blake feel guilty, and he didn't deserve that. He hadn't done anything wrong. But maybe his father had.

Years ago her mother had worked as a maid at Blake's parents' house. Then one day, she hadn't worked there anymore. Erin was young, but she remembered her mother crying. She remembered the anxiety, the tension. The fear. At the time she hadn't understood it fully. She still didn't understand it fully. All she knew was that something bad happened in that house when her mother had left.

"I just wish she would talk to me about it," she said, her voice thick with emotion. She and her mother had always been close, but her mother had never opened up about that time, even when Erin was old enough to have understood anything. And when Erin had finally confessed who Blake's parents were, her mother had seemed to shut down over the phone. At least after this visit they were going to visit her mother. Then she could see her in person and make sure everything was all right between them.

Blake's hands tightened on the steering wheel. "My parents are cold and manipulative. I'm not close to them, never have been. But I don't think they would have done…"

His voice trailed off, and they drove in silence for at least half a mile, watching light poles whip by.

Erin had never voiced her fear of what exactly might have driven her mother out of the house all those years ago. It could have been anything. There was no reason to assume it was something truly bad, like inappropriate behavior or even an assault. And yet she couldn't shake the possibility from her mind.

The fact that it would have been Blake's father who had done it made her stomach turn over. Not because she would blame Blake—she wouldn't. He hadn't even lived in the house at the time, having left for college and never returning. But because some part of her wondered if he'd believe, even *want* to believe her, if she somehow found out it were true.

The same thing had happened with her only other serious boyfriend. He'd said he didn't have a problem with what her mother did for a living. But when the truth had come out, that his father had come on to her mother, Doug hadn't believed her. Would the same thing happen again? She knew Blake was a better man than Doug, a stronger one, more honorable. But she couldn't be certain he would back her up if the choice was between her and his family. She never wanted to find out.

But she knew very well that history repeated herself. Blake himself had taught her that in his class.

"Erin." His voice had gone low. In warning? No, in worry.

Could he sense the distance between them? They were leaving his home but on some level it felt like leaving *them*, the way they were together, returning to who they were apart. "I don't want anything that happens to come between us," she said.

"God," he said, his voice rough. "No, it

won't. Of course it won't. I wouldn't let anything come between us."

That made her feel better, that he said it. That he clearly believed it. But she came from a world of leaky ceilings and broken dreams. She knew that wanting something to last wasn't enough. She knew that fighting for something didn't mean she'd get it.

She tried to smile. "I think I'm just overemotional. I didn't get enough sleep."

"That was my fault too."

"No," she said, horrified she'd said it that way. He would take the blame himself. He'd take the blame for everything if she let him. "You can't control the nightmares."

He shook his head, pushing aside what he'd see as excuses. "Rest, baby. Recline the seat and sleep. I'll wake you when we get there."

She wanted to argue, to make him see she didn't blame him. Not for last night, not for whatever his parents might have done. She wanted to tell him that nothing could break them apart. But with the seat lowered, sleep overcame her quickly.

She closed her eyes and dreamed.

BLAKE

THE ORNATE IRON gate rolled open before the car had come to a complete stop.

Blake nodded at the discreet security camera as he drove through. Whoever was manning the desk these days had obviously been informed of his impending arrival and recognized him. Mr. Henderson would have retired years ago, living off a stipend supplied by his parents. They took care of their servants. At least Blake had always thought so, despite whatever other flaws they had.

He intended to find out what happened with his father and the intern. He didn't want to believe his father was capable of that. He *didn't* believe his father was capable of it, but he would make sure. For Erin's sake.

He stopped the car at the end of the drive. His parents would have been informed of his arrival by the staff, but they wouldn't open the door until he knocked.

Erin was asleep, her lashes long on her cheeks, her pink lips slightly parted. She looked soft in the waning afternoon light, her skin almost glowing white against the orange horizon. Beautiful and untouchable and somehow vulnerable.

He suddenly didn't want to wake her up.

Didn't want to take her inside the house

where he'd grown up. Didn't want her exposed to whatever ugliness might have happened here. His father would never dare do anything to a guest, and Blake would never leave her side, but having her here felt wrong.

He hadn't moved, hadn't touched her, but she woke up anyway. Her eyes opened, deep brown and full of sleepy love for him. His heart thumped painfully against his chest.

"Hey," he said, his voice hoarse.

She smiled, her expression still dreamy. "You're thinking hard."

That made him smile too. "It's a character flaw."

"It's sweet." Wakefulness entered her eyes, along with worry. "Are you afraid I'll embarrass you in front of your parents?"

"What? Jesus, Erin. *No.*"

She sat up, using the lever to pull the chair upright. "I wouldn't blame you. I understand I'm not what they would have wanted for you."

He shook his head. He still couldn't believe what he was hearing. "I don't give a fuck what they want for me. You're what I want. You're what I need." The knot in his stomach grew tighter, and he couldn't ignore it. "We don't have to do this."

Her eyebrows dipped. "Do what?"

"Visit them. We can just leave. I'll tell them I wasn't feeling well." It wouldn't even be a lie at this point. He had a bad fucking feeling.

"No way. We're already here." She glanced out the windshield, her pretty eyes widening as she looked up and up. Because yeah, there were fucking spires, like a goddamn fortress. And it had been as cold as one when he was a kid, too. She swallowed. "We have to go in."

He knew that was true. He'd put off his visit long enough, knowing it was required, knowing that Erin would feel like he was ashamed if he didn't bring her. The best he could do was get it over with quickly. As far as he was concerned, after this, he was done. His parents could make a cameo at their wedding so the press wouldn't make a fuss, and that would be it.

He took her hand in his and kissed her palm. "Let's get this over with."

Chapter Twelve

Erin

Erin's first thought when a tall, grim woman opened the door: the Ice Queen. Her hair was a blonde so pale it was almost white, with no roots of course. She seemed naturally beautiful, effortlessly elegant, the kind of woman Erin had always envied. And her smile could put frost on the windows.

"You must be Erin," she said, taking her hand between long, cold fingers.

Erin forced a smile. "So glad to meet you, Mrs. Morris."

"I'm sure."

Blake's father wasn't much better. His hair a light grey, his eyes almost silver. At least in his case she had seen pictures online. The lauded ex-senator. Board member for countless charities. Successful investor. He was rumored to be a personal friend of the president, back in their fraternity days, and still had his ear. Yes, this family was steeped in money, and as they sat for lemonade in the sunroom, she felt the privilege thick and sharp.

"How was the drive?" his father inquired.

Blake's expression looked tense. Was he worried about what she would say? Or was he always this way around his parents? "Uneventful," he said. "Though we got a later start than we'd originally planned."

His mother made a tsking sound. "You've been away too long, and I don't just mean this morning. What can I tell people?"

"You can tell them you saw me now, mother. And that I'm getting married." With that, he gifted Erin a brief smile.

Unfortunately Mrs. Morris did not seem impressed with her. "I don't ask for much from you, Blake. You know that."

Well, that explained the tension. This had gone from awkward pleasantries to major parental guilt in the first fifteen minutes. She sent up thanks that her mother had only ever given love and support. She hadn't grown up with a father or a trust fund, but her childhood had been a hell of a lot warmer than this.

Blake sighed. "Mother, not now."

"When then?" She glanced at Erin, with

something almost like a sneer on her face. But that would be ugly, and this woman had never been ugly a day in her life. Erin imagined her waking up just as pretty, just as remote. "If she's going to be in this family, she should know the truth."

Erin froze, discomfort a hard knot in her throat. She'd been trying to ignore the truth, trying to pretend there was nothing to be uncovered here. Trying to pretend her mother had never dusted that lamp or swept this floor.

That way she could pretend she hadn't seen her mother crying, that she didn't wonder what had really happened in this house. Her gaze snapped to Mr. Morris, whose expression was unreadable. Was he angry? Bored? If nothing else, his poker face was to be admired.

"Erin and I are going upstairs now," Blake said, his voice and expression even. Had he learned that from his father? But it was clear he was upset. She could feel it in him as if they were connected. "We'll rest for a few hours and see you at dinner."

His mother sighed. "I'll have the maid show you to your rooms."

Erin was relieved at the prospect of leaving the house, even for a few minutes to get their bags from the car. But Blake followed a middle-aged woman in a simple black uniform up the stairs.

She stood for a moment at the base of the wide, curving staircase. Somehow this felt like crossing a threshold when just coming inside hadn't.

Blake paused, looking back. "You okay?" he asked softly.

"Coming," she answered, because she didn't feel okay. She didn't feel *not okay* either. She couldn't have described how she was feeling at all, so it was a relief when she took his hand and felt him squeeze.

They didn't need words to understand each other, to provide comfort. Didn't need words to take in the fact that they had been placed into separate bedrooms.

Apparently the word *rooms* had been plural on purpose.

"It's just how she is," Blake said after the housekeeper had gone. "Trying to exert control on what she can. We'll just move into one."

Erin surveyed the navy blue bedspread and classic baseball posters on the wall. It seemed impersonal and yet... it wouldn't be an ordinary guest bedroom. Not with that neat line of trophies on the bookshelf. "Was this *your* bedroom?"

He coughed. "We can stay in the other one."

"Oh no," she said, laughing. "We're definitely staying in this one."

His cheeks looked definitely darker. "The other room probably has a queen mattress. Maybe king. We'll have more room."

And his only had a double bed, it looked like, but she wouldn't have left for anything. Instead she wandered in, running her fingers along the smooth walnut desk and line of books. "What were you like as a kid?"

She was fascinated just thinking about it. He was so firmly adult in her mind, so experienced and even wise. This room did little to dispel that image. It was like something out of a catalog. Not lived in. Not *his*.

He snorted. "Selfish. Stupid. Like most kids in this neighborhood. Wait here and I'll get the bags from the other room."

The idea of a selfish Blake was as foreign to her as a young one. All kids were probably self-centered to some extent. Erin had been. That night her mother had come home crying had opened her eyes.

What had opened Blake's? His time overseas? Or something before that?

Blake returned with half the bags and stacked them by the others near the closet. She briefly wondered if Mrs. Morris would get upset about them messing with her room assignments, but Blake seemed to handle her pretty well.

"What do you want to do?" he asked, closing the door, shutting them in.

She shrugged. "Are you tired? You drove all that way, and I got to nap."

"A little. I could sleep, but only if you're with me."

The idea of sleeping in this bed together, in Blake's bed where he had been a teenager, where he had turned into a man, gave her a sort of thrill. There was an emotional component for sure, being with him, knowing him this way. As if the fabric, the mattress, had his story printed on them—invisible but just as true.

And there was a physical component too. A little taboo but definitely hot.

"I could lie down," she said, drawing her finger over the smooth bedding. "Though I wasn't thinking of sleeping."

Surprise flashed briefly through his eyes. "Here?"

She glanced back. Maybe smaller than their usual bed but definitely big enough for two.

"Have you ever?"

He knew what she was asking—if he'd ever had sex here before. An expression of guilt and pride crossed his face. "Yes."

She considered that, and what else she knew about teenage boys. "Where's your stash?"

His expression became suddenly, carefully blank. "My what?"

"Your stash. You know, stash of porn. Every boy has one, right?"

"What makes you think I left one here?"

She shrugged. "Did you?"

"I'd never leave something where my parents could find it."

"Oh." She was a little disappointed, but she searched for something else to ask him. It was too delicious being here where he'd once been both horny and innocent. They'd had sex a hundred times, a hundred ways—each time more inventive than the last. Was he always this way? Was it something he'd become? And then she knew what she'd ask next. "Who was your first?"

Silence.

She was sure he wouldn't answer. She'd crossed the line, gotten too personal.

And irrationally, she felt hurt. Weren't they going to share their lives together? God, she'd shared everything with him. Was she supposed to hold back?

He never let her hold back.

And the smile that crossed his face made her heart speed up. It was no longer vague or even shy, this smile. It promised that he wouldn't hold back either. When he reached back to lock the door, to lock them inside, she tensed. Because he wasn't just going to answer her with words.

And maybe that was what she'd wanted.

Then again, maybe it was more personal than she was ready for.

He leaned back against the door. "You want to know about my first time?"

She clenched the bedspread in her hand, rumpling the clean fabric, breaking the smooth lines. "I won't be jealous."

One eyebrow rose. "I didn't think you would be. No, I think you'll enjoy this story very much."

A shiver ran through her, her voice almost a whisper. "And why's that?"

He crossed the room, his long strides covering the room, and then he was in front of her, standing over her, dominating her with just a look. She loved the way he could affect her—body and mind. She craved it. And here, where it was probably inappropriate, where his parents were in the same house, where his mother didn't want them sleeping in the same bed much less fucking in the afternoon, she wanted it even more.

He lifted her chin. "We'll put on a show, beautiful. One for just you and me."

A show. She swallowed hard. Where he would play himself and she would play... this woman? This girl? This long ago memory who had once spread her legs for a cocky, selfish teenage boy upstairs in his room?

It was wrong to find this so hot, but her body clenched and tightened, ready to start, hungry for him.

When he bent his head to kiss her, she tilted up, meeting him halfway. Did the girl long ago do this? Was she as eager and as breathless as Erin felt now? And suddenly she had to know. She couldn't guess anymore.

"What did you do to her?" she asked.

"Shh," he said. "Lie back."

She wasn't sure whether he was going to answer or not, but she did as he asked anyway, reclining on top of the bedspread, kicking off her ballet flats as she went. She still had her clothes on—the same jeans and t-shirt she'd worn on the drive over. She'd only had a chance to use the restroom and splash water on her face when she'd arrived. She was far from fresh. Far from sexy. But the way he looked at her left no doubt as to his desire. The way his gaze scanned her body, with thoughtfulness, as if wondering the best ways to position her, left no part of her untouched.

"Her name was Clarissa," he said almost casually as he took his shirt off. In seconds the thin fabric was tossed to the floor, his broad chest bared to her. The lean slope of his abs took her breath away. Her gaze followed that line down, down—wanting to see more.

He didn't disappoint. He made quick work of his jeans, shucking them off, kicking them aside. He was all efficiency now. This wasn't a striptease, something slow and sensual. He was a man with a mission, and that made it even sexier to watch.

"She was a year older than me. A sophomore when I was a freshman. We went to the same prep school." He put one knee on the bed, making the old springs groan and dip. "She'd done it with one other guy before me."

She only had time to register that it was young to lose his virginity. Wasn't it? But then she didn't have a frame of reference. She'd helped her mother clean houses after class when she started high school. By the time she'd lost her virginity with Doug she'd been in college.

And then she was distracted by his hand on her knee. Just that. Almost innocent, that hand. He had put his fingers in her pussy and his tongue against her asshole. He had touched every part of her, but that hand on her knee just now, with them in his childhood bedroom, felt more illicit, more dangerous than anything that had come before.

He leaned down, his face just inches from hers. His eyes were large and dark—fathomless. She stared into them, losing herself.

Already lost.

"But you didn't want to hear about her," he whispered. "Not really."

"Then what did I want?" she whispered back.

He skimmed his palm up her thigh and caught her T-shirt as he went, lifting the fabric, baring her stomach to the cool air. Her skin pebbled, her nipples tightened. He noticed, his gaze hot as he watched the fabric of her bra peak.

Instead his large palm came up and covered her breast, over her bra—claiming her. That was how it felt, his hand both heavy and strong. Like she was no longer herself, her own person, but his. Like he was no longer her employer, her professor. Not even her lover.

Somewhere along the way he'd become her

everything, and that scared her more than anything.

"This," he said, locking his eyes on hers. "What you want is to know you can trust me, that I'm not this person. At least not anymore."

Her heart caught in her throat, because she did want that. Everything in this world was foreign to her, from the designer fixtures to the society page spreads. She didn't belong here.

And she was terrified he did.

"I don't want you to settle," she said, tears stinging her eyes.

BLAKE

BLAKE FORCED HIMSELF to close his eyes, to take deep breaths. Forced himself not to spread the beautiful legs beneath him and fuck Erin into the bed.

It was a strange impulse, but her words had that impact on him. That she could doubt herself that way, believe that she wasn't good enough. That she could doubt *him*. It made him feel primitive, called to some deep beastly part of him that needed to fight, to fuck, to conquer her until she saw what he did.

But he would keep that part of him contained, well hidden. He couldn't risk scaring her.

"Erin," he said, his voice low, almost guttural. "You're beautiful. You're strong. You're smart. Why the *fuck* would I be settling?"

She blinked rapidly. *Jesus.* So much for not scaring her.

He sat back on his heels and shoved a hand through his hair. Fuck, he was coming undone. Maybe it was coming home after so long. More likely it was the way Erin had looked at him ever since they'd gotten here, as if he were a stranger.

"Baby," he said hoarsely. Because he couldn't speak anymore.

He could only show her how he felt.

Only give in to the dark impulses that had been riding him all this time.

He bent over her, nuzzling at her breast through the satin cloth. God, he didn't even feel human now. More like an animal, acting on pure instinct and sensation, reveling in the softness and womanly scent of her. He used his teeth to drag the fabric aside, revealing her stiff nipple to the air. They were small nipples, delicate. He had to be careful with them. He couldn't suck as hard as he wanted, couldn't nip at her.

That was what he told himself, but one brush against his lips and he was lost, feasting on her, lips fastened on her breast and tongue tormenting her bud.

The sound she made was pain—a cry of shocked arousal and sharp desire.

He didn't let go of her, just cocked his head to meet her eyes. Then slowly, like a dog with a goddamn bone, shook his head. *Quiet,* he told her. She wouldn't want his parents or the staff to hear. There was no way to really hide what they were doing.

In the end she'd make enough sounds for them to know. But he wouldn't let her scream and keen the way she did at home. She'd only feel deeply embarrassed later.

So it was really a form of protection that when she yelped, he reached up to cover her mouth with his hand.

He'd bitten down, maybe too hard. He lightened up his hold on her sweet nipple, but he knew he would only be rougher with her. His control had gotten razor thin, almost a weapon in itself, something that could cut her even as he fought to keep her safe.

Her eyes grew wide with surprise. He'd never covered her mouth before. In his big house, far out in the rural wooded area, he'd never needed to.

Her breath was soft over his fingers as she breathed through her nose. She stared at him—bewildered, afraid. And turned on? Her breathing had sped up now, and he knew that she might be scared of him. Hell, she should be. But he also knew the rhythm of her body, the flush of her cheeks. He knew that being restrained, his hands on her wrists or his arm over her waist, could turn her on.

And it worked again, her hips pushing upward as her lips tested their newfound boundaries.

The sound she made was muffled.

He groaned, the sound hotter because he had controlled it. "That's right, baby. Give in to it. I'll make you feel good and I'll keep you safe while I do it. That's a goddamn promise."

Her body relaxed slightly, and he knew it was acceptance. More than that, desire.

And when he bent his head and tormented those pretty breasts, he didn't hold back. He made them shake, sucking her hard and then releasing. He marked the pale skin with the stubble on his cheeks, with his teeth. He used her flesh in every way he wanted, reveling in the soft sounds that slipped from beneath his hand.

He moved down her body, teasing and sucking the tender skin of her stomach, pushing her to the brink and then soothing her, quieting her again. To do what he wanted, to go where he wanted, between her legs, tasting her, he would need to remove his hand from her mouth. He didn't want to. Not when he knew how it affected her, when he'd felt her squirm under his body, felt the soft pants against his hand. She wanted this as much as he did—more. So when he finally released her, when he moved down her legs, taking her jeans and panties off as he went, he made a new plan.

Her panties were damp with arousal. He pressed the wetness to his mouth—a dirty kiss. Then he bunched the soft fabric and reached up.

Her lips parted, in surprise more than acceptance.

He used the opening anyway and pushed the fabric half into her mouth, a gag more effective than his hand, both more intimate and less, more tightly controlled and setting her free. Her body moved in a sinuous wave, painting shadows on her skin, giving only glimpses of her pink flesh. He longed to spread her wide. His dick throbbed, imagining that tight heat wrapped around him.

But he wouldn't do that to her. Couldn't do that to her.

Even in this state, half feral, he couldn't risk

scaring her with how he really felt.

So he gave himself time, by moving between her legs, by kissing her clit. He wasn't gentle, though. It was the one solace he gave himself, to fuck her with his tongue and his stubble and the graze of his teeth. She bucked up into him, her muffled moans a sweet music, humping his face until she keened out her release.

Liquid gushed onto his tongue and he swallowed it down. Only when he had drunk every drop of her pleasure, when he'd granted himself that reward, did he rise up and plunge inside.

She was slick and swollen and so well prepared. But even now she clenched hard around his intrusion, making him grunt in sweet agony. It felt too impossibly good inside her. It made him want to rut fast and hard, to finish as quickly as possible. But it also made him want to revel in slow, languid thrusts, making this sex last forever. It was a cruel paradox, one that had him pistoning his hips without any control at all, without any thought but to have her, take her, claim her.

Her eyes filled with tears, casting a strange and ethereal light. She looked like some kind of otherworld creature, a fairy come to torment him, come to save him. He was drunk on her, and on whatever magic made him this way—almost cruel.

Why did the sight of her lips stretched around her damp underwear make him wild? How did she make him crazed with just one fucking question?

Who was your first?

She was his first—the first woman he'd loved, the first woman he'd let in. The first woman to truly love him back, and he hated that she'd ever fucking doubted them.

It made him rough when he pushed inside her. Rough enough to hear her gasp. He tore the panties from her mouth so he could kiss her the way he wanted, deep and crude. He fucked her with his tongue the same way his dick thrust inside. He wanted her to taste her juices, to know that he was the one who had made her feel this way.

Only when she whimpered a final, softer orgasm did he let himself go. He pushed inside her again and again, almost fighting her, rough and hard and everything he shouldn't be. He fucked her like an animal—and that was how he came, with a roar that could be heard through the entire house.

He slumped over her, blanketing her with his body. She still shook slightly beneath him. Aftershocks? Or had he really hurt her?

He raised his head, and she smiled at him—so sleepy and full of love that his heart seemed to squeeze. He rolled over, bringing her with him, so she was sprawled on top of him. In minutes their breathing had evened out and matched up.

A soft snore, and he knew she was sleeping. It made him smile, but he was nowhere near sleep.

Who was your first?

As if the question was anything to do with a long-ago girl or the fact that she'd had braces and he'd been nervous out of his mind. No, the question was about the fear he'd seen in her eyes. The fear that he'd seen when she'd met his parents, seen their house. Maybe the fear had always been there and she'd just hidden it—or he'd just pretended not to see.

She still saw the class differences between them.

And he'd been an idiot not to see them too. Not that he believed himself above her in any way. But their childhoods had shaped them. He didn't want to think of himself as a pompous, self-entitled prick, but he couldn't deny that was exactly what he'd been raised to be. And no matter how hard he fought it, no matter how much he believed in equality, no matter how much he was head-over-fucking-heels in love with Erin, it could never change his past.

Chapter Thirteen

Erin

ERIN WOKE UP the next morning with an ache between her legs. It took a moment to remember what had happened yesterday—the long drive, the Ice Queen, the wild sex in Blake's childhood room.

After that there'd been an awkward dinner with only a long table and dim lights to hide her blush. Neither of Blake's parents had commented on their little nap, thank God.

And for whatever reason, his mother didn't launch into any more guilt tirades. Mostly she just drank martinis while Blake's father grilled him on his position at the university, his career plans, and his investment portfolio. Blake put up with it through the salad course and the main course before he persuaded his father to talk about political maneuvers from his heyday.

Once he got started Mr. Morris didn't stop talking. It was hugely interesting to listen to his stories, a front row seat to some of the major political dramas in their past. When Blake winked at her from across the table, she knew he'd done that on purpose.

What could she say? She had a weakness for men who could talk history.

If only she didn't know the senator's secret history.

Blake reclined beside her in bed. His arm was stretched out, long and muscled even in sleep. His eyes were closed, lashes thick and blunt, and almost touching the pale scar tissue on his cheek.

The fire had come too close to his eye. She shivered to think how much worse it could have been. He could have lost his sight. He could have died.

Her heart felt too full, too vulnerable after sleeping beside him all night.

And she couldn't stand to *not* touch him. Couldn't stand not to feel the warmth of him and the steady rise and fall of his breaths. His chest had a sprinkling of coarse hair, and she ran her hand over it, tickling her palm.

He didn't stir, his lips slightly parted in deep sleep.

So she kept going, over the ridges of his abdomen, feeling the muscles tighten under her touch. She glanced at him, feeling shy, almost caught, but he slept on.

There was no way she could stop, not when she could see him hard beneath the sheet. He probably woke up hard every morning, but usually he was up before her. Sometimes she'd open her eyes to find his fingers in her pussy and his mouth at her breast. Other times he'd already be inside her, thrusting away, by the time she became aware.

Still other times he would take a shower and jerk himself off, fast and efficient. *I wanted to let you rest,* he would say. And she understood it was a kindness, even if it didn't feel that way. Especially after days without him. Weeks. More than a month.

This was hers. His cock. His arousal. This entire beautiful man was hers.

That was how it felt to take his cock into her mouth—like ownership. She claimed him with her lips, her tongue, with the gentle strokes of her fist around his cock.

His gasp was like coming up for air, sharp and sudden. His whole body jerked too, hard enough that her mouth left him. Then his hand was on the back of her head, caressing her, thanking her. She licked him at the tip, in that place that always drove him crazy, until he shoved his fingers into her hair, tugging and wordlessly begging.

He couldn't keep quiet, though. Not when she licked at the soft skin on his balls, her fist tightening on his cock to make sure he didn't come yet. She'd gotten good at this with him. She loved to practice, loved to make him crazy with it, and he responded with a symphony of arousal— his grunts, his groans, his gasped words of encouragement and pain.

"God, baby. Suck me. I need you so fucking bad."

Her pussy clenched at his words, and she obeyed him, taking him into her mouth again. She fisted him in time with her sucks, and he tossed his head back, eyes closed, expression tight.

"Baby," he muttered. "Need this. Need you."

He was holding back. She could tell he wanted to say more, to ask for something she might not want to give. What he didn't know was that she wanted to give him everything. Her only fear was that he'd realize he no longer wanted her.

"Tell me," she whispered, her lips brushing the spongy head of his cock.

"Nothing," he gasped, bucking up. "This is perfect. Love you. Love you."

But it wasn't perfect. Not if he was still holding back. She blew a breath over the tip of his cock, and he shuddered. "What do you want to do to me?"

"Want to fuck your mouth." Then he seemed to realize what he said, and added, "Don't want to scare you though."

He wanted to fuck her mouth? The idea made her hot. He usually let her control the pace, the depth. She'd never really questioned why.

Apparently because he didn't want to scare her.

"You won't scare me," she promised.

He stared at her, his eyes dark and wondering. She could see his hesitation in those eyes, but she could also see how much he wanted this.

"Not like this," he finally said. "Lie down."

She lay down, uncertain what he meant until he knelt over her, her arms trapped at her sides, her mouth inches from his cock. It was a startling perspective, being towered over by him, by the closeness of his cock and his shoulders blocking the light from the window, his face cast in shadows.

And it made her a liar, because it scared her— just a little.

But she knew that however dominating he might seem, however vulnerable this made her, he would never hurt her. Maybe that was what love was really about. Feeling fear but knowing it would be all right. Maybe that was trust. She'd always longed for safety, the certainty that she would never be alone, never crying, never somehow hurt by her employer but without the power to defend herself the way her mother had been.

There was no such thing as certainty. That was what she'd learned by growing up, by reading about the world, by studying history. There was only pain and hope, only fear and trust, only the hard cock in her mouth and the tender look from a man who loved her.

"Is this okay?" he asked, his voice hoarse.

She nodded, unable to speak. He wasn't deep yet, but she felt full. And trapped. Perfectly contained from both inside and out, held on a single breath.

"I'm going to start slow," he promised.

And he kept his promise, of course he did. He rocked his hips, pushing deeper into her mouth. Once she felt him at the back of her throat, when it was almost too far, he pulled back. Again and again, he fucked her mouth. Just like he'd promised. Just like he needed.

His whole body seemed to tremble with the

restraint, but he didn't go faster or harder. He didn't hurt her. "Baby, you're so fucking hot. So wet. Like a goddamn dream."

All she could do was blink up at him. And use her tongue in grateful response.

He gasped. "Jesus. I want to go deeper. You can take it."

She lowered her lashes to her cheeks, breaking eye contact, because she wasn't sure she could. Her lips were already stretched apart. He already brushed the back of her throat when he pushed in. It wasn't all of him, but she wasn't sure how much more she could take.

His voice was soft with understanding. "You can do this, baby. Just give me a couple more inches. I need you to nod for me. I won't take it."

Nerves raced down her spine, but she wanted to do this. She nodded.

After studying her for a moment, he pushed deeper. "Now, baby. Relax for me."

Then he pushed deeper still, and when he would have stopped before, pulled back, he kept going instead. For an awful second she fought the intrusion. Even with her eyes locked on his, knowing he was going to be gentle, she struggled to get her arms free, to push him away.

Just as quickly the moment passed and she

was able to relax.

He held himself there for three beats and then pulled out slowly, letting her breathe again. She gasped for air around his cock.

"One more time," he said gently. "Tell me yes."

But she couldn't, not with his cock still in her mouth, so she only nodded. And then he was deep in her again, the short hair at his base tickling her nose. She held herself still until the sensation in her throat made her swallow. He groaned loud and rough, then swore under his breath.

"Fuck, baby. Fuck."

He was already coming as he pulled out, his first load already down her throat, and just a faint salty flavor on her tongue. Then his body jerked and he spurted into her mouth, right to the back of her throat. She swallowed him down eagerly while he groaned above her.

He pulled away gingerly, careful not to hurt her. But she was beyond pain now. All she felt was the throbbing in her pussy.

"Shh," he soothed. "Let me take care of you."

Tears sprang to her eyes. "I need... I need..."

Her voice was too hoarse, and she didn't know how to say it anyway. Didn't know how to explain that she'd go insane if she didn't come in two seconds flat.

Instead she grabbed his hand and pressed it between her legs—the move crude and telling. His expression softened with understanding.

His fingers dipped between her pussy lips, where she was impossibly slick for him. He gathered wetness and drew it up to her clit, sliding around the hard nub, making her clench her legs. It was too much, her flesh too sensitive. But at the same time she wanted him harder, faster.

He shifted to kiss her lips, the soft press a sharp contrast to the invasion of his cock. He said again, "Let me take care of you."

He moved so that his thumb was beside her clit. It was almost a pinch—and then she was beyond thought, moaning as she came, bucking against him.

She had only just collapsed back onto the bed when the door swung open.

She squeaked in embarrassment and horror. Before she could fully process the Ice Queen at the door, Blake had thrown the sheet on her.

"Jesus," he said.

"Don't swear. How was I to know you would be in bed at this hour?"

There was a pause where she imagined him

shaking his head. "Give us a minute, mother. Or sixty of them."

The door closed again, and Erin remained hidden under the sheet. She knew her cheeks would be bright red. God, talk about embarrassing. That wasn't even the kind of story she could tell people about as a joke.

Footfalls crossed the floor followed by a small sound, and she knew Blake was locking the door. The bed dipped as he sat beside her.

Finally he tugged at the sheet.

After a moment, she reluctantly peeked over the edge.

"I'm sorry. I should have locked it last night."

"Your mom..." She trailed off, unsure of where to go with that. Obviously there were issues here. And while she wasn't a big fan of his mother, and it didn't seem like he was either, she didn't want to offend him by saying the wrong thing.

"She's always been a little... invasive. I'm just sorry I didn't protect you better from it. I'm used to it, I'm just pissed she did it to you."

"No, it wasn't your fault." And he *had* protected her. Now she understood why he hadn't brought her. It wasn't embarrassment of her like she'd feared. If anything he seemed embarrassed for her to see where he came from.

A rush of tenderness made her lower the sheet and take his hand. "Don't worry about it," she said. "Really. We'll just get through today and leave tomorrow."

He shook his head ruefully, looking down at his naked body. "At least now she can't complain about not seeing enough of me."

And when Erin laughed, she knew they would be okay.

Whatever happened, they had each other.

BLAKE

BLAKE LEANED BACK. The antique chair whimpered under his weight, clearly ready to retire after probably seventy years of service. Everything in this house was old, from the walls themselves to the Ming vases against the wall. He remembered not sitting on this chair as a child. He remembered not touching those vases, not drawing on these walls. He'd almost grown up in a museum, learning from a young age not to touch, to move, to speak above a whisper.

Enlisting had been half about rebellion, half about finding his place in the world out of his father's shadow. And it had blown his ideas about everything apart. Soldiers constantly moved and fought and shouted. It was the exact opposite of everything he'd known before.

He'd left the army a broken man, and the worst part, the sickest part, had been the look of veiled triumph in his parents' eyes. That he'd set out to do something for himself, something different from what they'd wanted him to be, and he'd failed.

Rebuilding himself had been a slow painful process. Painful, because the burn scars would be there forever, always restricting his movement and sending sharp pain into his skin. Slow, because he'd fought with himself the whole way. Only when he'd met Erin, when he'd fallen in love with her, when he'd needed to be good enough for her, had he been able to step out of his own way.

The pain would never go away, not completely. And it would be a long road for him.

But he had the most beautiful woman he'd ever seen at his side, a woman so smart and kind and good that he no longer cared if he was deserving. He would keep her, and in that way, she would become the best part of him.

Erin sat across the room from him playing chess with his father.

And winning, judging by the surprised look

on his father's face. He wasn't bested often, at least partly because people were intimidated by him. Erin was intimidated, Blake knew, but that only drove her harder. His chest grew tight, a mixture of pride and love—and undeniable lust. It turned him on when she kicked ass.

"Check," she said.

Curious, he stood and crossed the room. "She has your king on the run," he commented idly.

Of course his father would know that. "Indeed. Did you teach her that?"

"That particular trick she already knew." He studied the board while his father moved in defense. Erin moved quickly after that, on the offense, using her bishops in tandem to sweep his father's pieces across the board. "She has a way of winning a man over."

A small smile crossed Erin's face. "Man or woman, I play to win. Check."

His father studied her with new and cautious respect after his king moved back again. "You know most young people would have humility. They'd say it was probably just luck to have bested me."

"It's not luck." She reached over to place her knight. "So why lie? Checkmate."

His father studied the way he'd gotten trapped

on the board—and the way she'd almost hidden the knight behind a rook, so that in his hasty, single-minded retreat, he hadn't noticed until it was too late. "I'll be damned."

"It's okay," Blake said. "I felt the same way when I met her."

Well, not exactly the same. He'd also felt arousal so intense it had jolted him back to the land of the living, when he'd thought himself almost past desire.

"Tell me your strategy," his father said, in that imperious way he had that made people fall at his feet.

Erin shrugged. "You rely too much on your queen. Most people do. It leaves your king vulnerable."

That earned her an eyebrow raise. Then his father turned to Blake. "She's a lovely young woman. And smart too. Probably even smarter than you."

"Definitely."

"Well, you made a good choice. I wish you both a long and happy life."

Blake's chest ached, because he wanted more than anything for that to be the truth, for his father to be a stern and emotionally remote but ultimately good man. But he couldn't ignore what

Erin had told him. He deserved for her sake, for her mother's sake—even for his own sake, to know the truth about what had happened here.

He lowered his voice. "Could I speak with you a moment?"

His father's forehead creased. "Yes. In my office."

"We'll just be a few minutes," he told Erin, hoping she'd understand why he had to leave her alone for a few minutes. He wouldn't have left her with his father… not after reading her thesis. But he needed to get some answers.

Her pretty brows drew together. "Of course. Take your time. I'll be here."

"You can go upstairs and take a nap." He doubted she would sleep, but at least then she could be in a somewhat private place while he was gone.

"Maybe." Her smile was fleeting.

He didn't like leaving her this way, with words left unspoken between them, but now was the time if he was ever going to confront his father about this. So he gave her a quick kiss on her forehead. "We'll be quick," he promised.

Chapter Fourteen

Erin

Erin stared at the empty doorway where Blake had just been. What was that about? He'd been quiet after lunch, sitting apart from them while they'd played chess. The Ice Queen had disappeared to "take a nap" after lunch, though Erin was beginning to understand that was the term used in this house for anything private.

Suddenly she heard footsteps. Was Blake back already? He'd said they would be quick.

But these didn't sound like his footsteps.

Blake's mother appeared in the doorway. The Ice Queen. *Shit.* She wished desperately that she'd agreed to take a nap when Blake had offered. Then she wouldn't be sitting here like a… like a sitting duck, actually.

Which made Blake's mother the hunter.

"There you are, sweetheart. Where are the boys?"

"I think they went to Mr. Morris's study."

"Oh." Mrs. Morris moved deeper into the room, a faint smile on her face. "You know you can call him Jeb. And call me Bel."

Erin knew their names were Jebediah and Belinda. Old names. Beautiful names. The people themselves were both old and beautiful—and intimidating too. She had no desire to be here, alone with Bel, with the Ice Queen, and maybe that was unfair of her.

Maybe the woman was good at heart, with hopes and dreams and fears of her own. Undoubtedly that was true. But she couldn't shake the feeling that she had singled out Erin as her enemy. And something told her Bel was a dangerous enemy to have.

"You know, Blake suggested that I go take a nap, and now that I think about it, I am tired. I think I'll go—" Erin stood up and gave a pretend-stretch to make the point.

"Stay." Bel smiled again, sending a shiver down her spine. Her tone left no room for discussion. "You're only here for tonight, after all. So little time to get to know you."

Erin forced herself to sit back down in her chair while Bel sat down on the antique-style sofa nearby. Very nearby. There were only inches between their knees, and it made Erin uncomfortable. Was she overreacting? Probably. But knowing that didn't shake the tightness in her chest, the dread in her throat.

Maybe she could still fix this. If she used the same tactic Blake had used with his father. "I'd love to hear about your life," she said, feigning enthusiasm. "I'm sure you have lots of stories as the wife of a senator."

Bel laughed. "Oh, I do. Stories about Jeb… you wouldn't believe some of them, I'll bet. They would shock you. Or maybe they wouldn't. You seem like a girl who understands the world and its darker sides."

That sounded ominous. She tried to steer the conversation back to lighter topics. Maybe flattery would help. "You must have gotten to meet some important people."

"I have, darling. But I'm much more interested in you."

She swallowed. "Me? I'm afraid I haven't done much that's interesting."

"Haven't you? You already snagged Blake Morris, after all."

Erin stared, unsure what to say. What to feel. Technically it was true. She'd snagged Blake, who was a catch. Smart, kind, and hot as hell despite what he thought about his scars. Of course any mother would think that her son was a prize. And yet, she couldn't help think Bel was talking about Blake's money more than anything else.

"I'm glad to be with him," she said carefully. "I love him."

The smile seemed a little sinister but no less beautiful. "Of course you do. They're lovable, our Morris men."

What did that mean? "I think so," she said, hoping that was the right answer. There were undercurrents here she couldn't see. She could only feel them.

"Some might say too lovable. I'm sure you know what I mean."

Erin was sure she didn't. She would also rather be anywhere but here. The doorway beckoned her, and she wanted to run right through it and hide upstairs—except that would be childish.

It also seemed like a smart option.

"They'll be out any minute," she said in a rush, almost a prayer. Because God, she hoped so.

Bel didn't even acknowledge that. Her eyes narrowed. "The important thing, with men like that, is to know where their loyalty lies."

Well, this was getting unnerving. "Okay," she

said. "That's good advice. Now I really think I'm going to head upstairs and take that nap."

"Do you know where Blake's loyalty lies, Erin?"

She knew she was being baited. And yet she couldn't help but respond. "Blake wouldn't cheat on me, if that's what you mean."

"Maybe not. You're young and pretty, and he's... well, he's not quite the man he was. Some injuries can never be repaired."

Excuse me? Shit just got real. She may not have known the man Blake was, but she knew the man he was now. "I don't know what you're talking about, but Blake is an amazing man. He's honorable and brilliant and—"

"And fifteen years older than you. You aren't fooling anyone, sweetheart. Definitely not him. He knows what he's got in a pretty little co-ed with a crush on the professor."

Erin gasped. She didn't want this woman to mess with her head, but that was her fear. Not that she was using Blake, but that he'd think so. Not that she didn't truly love him, but that he didn't truly love her. *No,* she wouldn't let Bel mess with her. "You're obviously angry and bitter over something, but you don't know me. And I'm thinking you don't know him."

"I know enough. I know he's rejected everything we've ever stood for, including a life in politics, including our friends, including the kind of woman who would have been a good wife to him. Instead he'd picked you, in some kind of adolescent rebellion."

"I *will* be a good wife."

"And I know you came from trash. That's all you'll ever be."

BLAKE

BLAKE DIDN'T LOOK forward to spending time in this office, where he'd been lectured many times for some dumbass antic or another. He had quite a rap sheet at the prep school he'd gone to— ironic considering he was now a professor.

His father didn't sit behind his desk. Instead he sat in one of the high-back leather armchairs by the fire, and Blake joined him there. Equals? Blake doubted that would ever be true. And maybe that was the way of fathers and sons, for one always to be the leader, even if the son had stopped following years ago.

"It must be serious," his father remarked idly. "If it's taking you this long to come out with it."

Blake huffed a laugh without humor. "Serious, yes. I have a question to ask you, but I'm afraid I won't like the answer."

His father was silent, staring into a fire grate with no fire. Long minutes passed. "I know you thought I hated that you enlisted. And you're right. I did."

"Glad we cleared that up," Blake said dryly.

"I was scared. Scared you'd never come home. And I was right, in a way. You never did come back to us."

His throat was dry. "It wasn't me you wanted. It was some other kid. One just like you."

"Not just like me. I never had your courage."

There was a finality to his words that made Blake's gut clench. "I didn't cut you out completely. I'm here now. And you'll be invited to the wedding."

"Even if you don't like my answer to this question you're going to ask?"

It was Blake's turn to be silent, because he couldn't make any promises. His loyalty was to Erin, and beyond that, it was to do the right thing. Any gratitude he had for his parents was like this house—old and creaking under the weight of the present.

"Dad, what happened with the intern in Washington?"

Silence. Stillness. His father had heard him, and understood him, every nuance of the question. He didn't bother pretending not to know or asking *which intern?* There must have been a hundred interns over the course of his congressional career.

Blake gave him time to answer, because he'd rather have the truth. And he knew that for all that his father could spin a lie, in this room with just the two of them, he'd hear it.

His father spoke slowly. "How do you know about that?"

"Does it matter how I found out?"

"I suppose it doesn't." A slow shake of his head. "You were at university then, and coming home as rarely as possible. I thought you'd follow in my footsteps, but even then, you would hardly come to my office. You never met her."

Suspicion turned dark. "Why would you remember that? Something so specific, about an intern meeting your son?"

"Because she wasn't just an intern."

Blake closed his eyes. "So it's true."

"It was wrong. I'm not defending myself. I'm just answering your question."

"Did you hurt her?" he demanded. "Did you…" He couldn't even say the word. "Did you *force* her?"

"What?" His father turned to him, a rare shocked expression on his lined face. "Christ, no. I would never force *anyone*, never hurt any woman. And definitely not her."

"Jesus." He supposed his father could lie to him, but Blake believed him. An affair with an intern was still bad, but not as terrible as forcing a woman. "Do you know what Erin's thesis was about?"

A muscle ticked in his father's jaw. "She's the one who told you?"

"She didn't tell me a damn thing. Probably because she knows it would hurt me." Though there was a darker possibility—that she thought he wouldn't believe her. "I had to request a copy of her thesis from a colleague. That's how I found out."

"I cared for that girl. A great deal."

"That girl? How old was she?"

"Old enough. I think that's a stone you can't throw, considering who you brought home."

"I wasn't a senator. She wasn't my intern."

"You were her professor. And her employer. Give me some credit. You may not call and give me regular updates, but I care about what happens to my son."

Blake's stomach churned. Had he become my father after all? The worst parts of him, the part that would use a woman for sex. That would intimidate her. "What happened to her?"

"Your mother found out. She didn't confront me, though. She waited until I was out of town and then confronted the girl. It was…a bad situation. I blame myself."

"No shit," Blake said, his voice hard.

"By the time I got back and realized what happened…" His father sighed, looking more tired than he'd ever been. "It was too late. Your mother had spread the rumor that she slept with me, and there went any chance of her having a career in Washington. The worst part is that I couldn't refute it. No, that's a lie. I could have tried. I didn't stand up for her."

Blake agreed but he was too sick over the whole thing to say so. In the end he understood the irony of him accusing his father of wrongdoing. Blake had fought his attraction to his young maid, knowing it was too improper, that she was too young and beautiful and good for him. And in the end he had given in to his desire—just like his father.

There were differences too. Blake wasn't married. He hadn't broken any vows to be with Erin.

And when it came to defending her against anyone, he would fight a fucking army.

His father sighed. "Our marriage had its issues. I can't even say it was the first time I strayed, but it was the only time that meant anything. Your mother somehow knew that. It changed her. She became more bitter. More angry. God, keeping the assault charge under wraps became a full-time job for a while."

"The assault charge?"

My father looked grim. "Yes. That's why she waited for me to leave. She didn't just confront the girl. She slapped her. Pulled her hair so hard she bled."

"Holy fuck."

"I told her." His eyes darkened with pain. "When I got back, I told her it was my fault. Mine. She couldn't stop blaming the girl. And blaming every young woman who slept with an older man, as if it wasn't my goddamn fault for touching her."

Was that why his mother was so cold to Erin?

Was it why she walked in on them having sex this morning?

He had left Erin in the living room undefended. If his mother was determined to hurt Erin, this was the perfect opportunity. He needed to find her. Now.

Chapter Fifteen

Erin

ERIN'S FIRST DATE came in her junior year. Already she was a late bloomer. Her other friends had already been asked—but they also had time to hang out at the mall for hours and attend the football games. Erin worked between ten and fifteen hours a week with her mother. So when one of the cutest boys in school had not only noticed her, but asked her to a movie Saturday night, she'd spent fifteen dollars on a cute new top and wore her favorite jeans.

The night went perfectly. They laughed together, they held hands. She fell as quickly as it was possible to fall, then they drove out to the make-out point. She was still on board. She wanted him to kiss her, to touch her. She didn't want to have sex.

"Come on, Erin," he'd said, frustrated. "I paid for the movie and popcorn. And now you're acting shy? All I want is to touch you. Are you a fucking tease?"

She'd been torn between shame and anger and a desperate wish for acceptance. So she'd let him pull off her new top and grope her breasts. She'd let him pull her face to his lap. He'd humped her mouth until he came, spurting across her tongue and her lips.

Ever since then she'd tried to live honestly, to say no when she really meant it, to only say yes when she wanted to. And definitely never to trade sex for safety, for influence, for money, letting herself be bought. She'd always wanted to have sex with Blake.

And she believed he'd always wanted her.

It was hard to remember that in the face of the Ice Queen calling her trash.

"You come from nothing. You *are* nothing. Scars or not, he could find a woman with a goddamn pedigree. So why would he want a young, pretty girl who knows no one?"

Her cheeks burned. Is that what had happened? Had she let him pay for a movie and popcorn—and then let him push her face to his lap? No, she didn't believe that. "I don't know why you're trying to come between us, but it won't work."

"I'm not trying to come between you, I just

want to be honest with you. Women like you, you get ideas about men like Blake. That they'll marry you, that they'll leave their families for you." Bel stood up, looming over her. "But they won't."

Erin tried to stand, but Bel was blocking her with her body—and was surprisingly strong for her thin frame. The older woman clamped a hand on her wrist.

Erin was too shocked to fight her off. "Let go of me," she whispered.

Bel twisted her fist, sending pain down Erin's arm. "When push comes to shove, they don't want you. They want me. Women like you are just good for a *fuck*."

Erin wasn't sixteen anymore. She was a grown woman, and she was strong, and she wouldn't cower and let herself be hurt even if she would be rejected by the man she loved in the end. She yanked herself free, sending Bel sprawling on her knees. "I *said* let go of me," she said with remarkable calm. "And don't ever speak to me that way again."

Blake appeared in the doorway. "What the hell did she say?"

As Erin looked from Bel on the floor to Blake and Jeb standing in the doorway, shocked, she couldn't even speak. It was too awful. She was too much the outsider here. Too much like Bel had described. Young and pretty, only good for a fuck.

She started to leave, pushing past Blake.

He caught her wrist, and she winced, cradling her arm close.

His eyes widened. "Did she *hurt* you?"

"It doesn't matter," she said, her voice too wobbly to be believed. "I just want to go. I need to... I need to leave. Don't worry about me."

"How dare you." He practically roared at his mother. "How dare you put your hands on her. How dare you even *speak* to her."

His mother didn't stand up, barely even looked up. Wouldn't meet his eyes. "She's a little tramp, Blake. Everyone can see it. It's embarrassing, you bringing you here."

"She doesn't exist to you. Not anymore. And neither do I." Blake turned to her, his expression like stone. "Go upstairs and pack. I'll meet you there in a few minutes."

He was going to continue defending her, and judging by the dark look in his eyes, it was going to be awful. Awful enough to ruin any chance of reconciliation between him and his parents. Even if he didn't mind that thought now, he might eventually. She wouldn't be responsible for that. She couldn't.

"Please," she begged. "Come with me. Take me away from here."

Jeb stepped forward, his eyes somber. "Take care of her. She's the most important. Your mother and I will have words. Don't make the same mistakes I did."

Blake looked torn. He gently pushed a piece of hair out of Erin's eyes. "She can't treat you that way. We should call the cops. Press charges."

"I didn't let her," Erin said. Her voice grew stronger. "I stood up for myself, but now I just want to leave. There's nothing for me here. The cops can't help me now."

He took her in his arms, careful as if he knew she might be sore. And she was, though more in her heart, than from anywhere his mother had touched. "My beautiful, brave girl. Let's go. Let's get you out of here."

BLAKE

BLAKE DROVE WITHOUT any idea where he was going.

Their original plan had been to spend one more night at his parent's house. Then they'd head to Erin's mother's house in the morning. Instead they'd hastily packed their bags and tossed them in the trunk. It was nine o'clock at night, and he was barreling down the highway without a plan.

It occurred to him that he might not be in a good frame of mind to drive. He saw the road, but it was mostly a blur. A dark blur. Well, he wasn't about to ask Erin to drive—not after she'd been berated and insulted. Not after she'd been fucking *assaulted.*

God, he still couldn't believe his mother had gone that far.

It was despicable. It was unforgivable. It was a wonder Erin had even gotten in a car with him after what he'd subjected her to, but then again, it had been the fastest way out of that house. Had he lost her now? Had he really managed to fuck up the best thing in his life with one small, final act of loyalty to a family that didn't deserve it? He should never have brought her for a visit.

He found himself pulling off on a familiar exit. He'd driven this way so many times that it felt like second nature, even though it had been years now. The manicured plots and bright storefronts quickly gave way to a dark, tree-lined road. It might even be spooky if he didn't know how cheery the dappled black concrete and yellow stripes looked in the daylight.

He had no idea what Erin thought about this turn of events. She hadn't spoken much since they'd left, just a few nods and murmurs when required.

"Away," had been her answer, when he'd asked her where she wanted to go.

He didn't like the idea of driving to Sofia's house tonight. For one thing, it would take a few hours, so they'd be exhausted by then. For another, Sofia wasn't expecting them, so it might inconvenience her. And lastly, he didn't want to force Erin to confront her mother when she seemed somehow fragile. He knew they were close—definitely nothing like his relationship with his parents—but this particular issue hit a little close to home.

And so, he found himself heading toward Lover's Point, a plateau with a great view of the city. By day it was visited by hikers along a five-mile trail. By night it served as the premier make-out spot.

He had no plans to make out with her. Even though she'd never been more beautiful, more desirable to him, she also seemed somehow untouchable. Ephemeral in the moonlight coming through the window, her skin pale and eyes fathomless.

Plus he couldn't trust himself to be gentle right now.

Not with his rage so close to the surface. Still, it would be a quiet place they could sit and talk. If Erin would even talk to him.

The car bumped along the dirt path—well traveled by high schoolers, including himself, but still plenty uneven after every rain. All the cars, all the years, couldn't smooth out a land this ancient. When he reached the grassy clearing, he stopped the car.

The city stretched out in front of them, a blanket of lights to a city already abed.

"It's beautiful," Erin said, her voice soft.

He couldn't even look directly at her, because she made his chest tight and his face tight and his body tight. All he could do was look out at the city. "Yes."

"Thank you for bringing me here."

She was thanking him? No, he needed to be on his fucking knees, thanking her for being with him, for staying with him, thanking her for fucking existing—because she was his light. Not a single one in that city shone for him. Only the woman sitting next to him lit up a damn thing.

"Baby," he said. "We need to talk about what happened."

"Do we?" She sounded sad, almost lost.

"We do, because you need to know that it was not okay, that I don't support what happened in any way, that I wish to hell I'd gotten back to you a few minutes sooner so I could have put a stop to it myself."

"I know."

"I would never allow her to disrespect you in my presence, and I'm sick over the fact that I did allow it, by not realizing it would happen, by not being there for you."

She put her hand on his. "Blake, I know."

He pulled himself together enough to realize she'd had to repeat herself. He turned his hand over to hold hers. "How can you be okay with this?"

"I'm not okay with what happened. But it wasn't your fault. You couldn't have predicted she'd act like that. And once you realized, you got me out of there."

He studied her arm, looking for any signs of bruising. It was too shadowy in the car to see. "Where did she hurt you?" When she seemed reluctant to answer, he added, "I need to know."

"She grabbed my wrist, that's all."

"That's all? That's a big fucking deal."

"I didn't mean to... okay, yeah, I meant to

216

downplay it. I just meant I'm fine. It will be tender for a little while. No medical intervention required."

He still didn't like how casual she was being about being manhandled, but he recognized she wanted to drop the subject. And short of taking her to an emergency room, which would be more traumatic for her, there wasn't anything else he could do.

He ran a hand through his hair. "I read your thesis."

That got her attention. Her eyes widened, two dark ponds in the night.

"That's what I was talking to my father about. According to him, it was an affair. A consensual affair. He claims to have cared about her, the intern. But when my mother found out, things got ugly, as he put it. I guess we saw a taste of that today."

"God," she breathed. "I'm sorry. I didn't want you to know."

"My father has done some brave things in his lifetime. Even though I didn't get along with him, I looked up to him, knowing what he'd accomplished. But in that moment, he was a coward. He didn't stand up for the woman he cared for, didn't protect and defend her."

She squeezed his hand gently until he met her eyes again. "You're not him," she said softly. "You did defend me. You always protect me."

He let out a breath. "Jesus, Erin. I want that to be true."

"It is true. You're strong and capable and incredibly intelligent. And you use all of that, the entire force of you, to make my life better. Sometimes I don't feel... deserving."

Suspicion formed in his gut. "Is this what my mother said?"

Erin looked away. "Some of it. Maybe I was already worried."

"Erin," he said, putting steel into his words. He knew this was uncomfortable for her, but he needed to know what had been said. Especially since it made Erin like this, curled up and somehow ashamed.

Instead of answering, Erin opened the car door and stepped outside. She might have murmured something like "need some air" but she didn't pause to make sure he'd heard. The car door slammed shut, and he was quick to follow her into the night.

He wouldn't push her to talk. He realized that much. If there was a risk she would run away from him, he would just have to live without fucking knowing what his mother had said to upset and hurt her.

She stood looking out over the city, and he was struck with a sense of déjà vu for all the nights he had woken up from a nightmare. They hadn't been sleeping but in essence that was what Erin had just done—woken up from a nightmare. Her arms were wrapped tightly around her middle, warding off the cool breeze. Her gaze was far away, unseeing.

He came to her from behind, putting his arms around her. He held her gently and kissed the top of her head, the same way she had kissed the middle of his back.

"You okay?" he murmured.

"Getting there." She twined her arms over his, locking them together. "This is helping."

"Good." The night air was cool, borderline cold, but soothed him. Still he pulled her in close to keep her warm. "We can find a decent motel on the highway. Stay the night, then head to your mother's as planned in the morning. Does that sound okay?"

"Sure." She sighed. "I mean, it sounds like a really good plan. Sorry I'm kind of distracted."

"Christ, Erin, you keep apologizing."

"Sorry, I—" She laughed. "I'll stop."

He shook his head, a slight smile on his face. God, this woman. He couldn't get enough of her. He wanted to hold her, breathe her in. In all honesty, he wanted to fuck her. He was hard as the fucking rocks around them. Apparently his body hadn't gotten the message about extreme emotional distress. Or actually it had gotten the message, but it interpreted his adrenaline rush as arousal. Here he was, holding the most beautiful, sexy woman he'd ever known—and his dick had no idea why it couldn't be in her. He cleared his throat and took a half step back to make sure she wouldn't feel the erection against her back.

When she rocked her hips back in a sensual, knowing sway, he knew it was too late. She already knew. Now wasn't the right time. She was vulnerable and hurt. He shouldn't touch her. But her body invited him in with a soft moan he barely heard over the crickets and the pounding of his heart, and he was helpless to refuse.

CHAPTER SIXTEEN

ERIN

ERIN TURNED IN Blake's arms.

She knew they had things to work through. Important things, like whatever doubts she still harbored that had let Bel mess with her head. They needed to talk about them and deal with them... but right now she didn't have the strength for that.

She'd used all she had standing up for herself and holding her head up high in the few minutes it took them to leave the house. And Blake's arms felt too good—warm and strong and secure. Like she could let go and be completely safe.

And so that was all she wanted to do, let go in the most carnal way, to pant and rock and fuck until she'd lost all thought, until her body was a mindless mass of pleasure.

Blake's eyes were dark with concern. "Are you sure—"

She silenced him with a hand on his cock. He

was already hard as steel in his jeans. She rubbed the taut denim, savoring his rough groan. "Are you?" she asked.

She didn't mean sex. She meant sure about them. About their marriage. She meant all the deep things she hadn't wanted to discuss yet.

He grunted and closed his eyes. "Fuck yes."

He might have meant sex or he might have meant everything. It didn't matter. *Right answer.*

She made quick work of his jeans, unzipping them and shoving them down his hips. His cock sprang out, thick and heavy in her hands. "Someone might see," he warned.

"Let them." She wanted them to see, the whole city watching. She wanted everyone to know that Blake Morris was hers. And most of all, she needed to show herself it was still true.

He groaned, leaning down for a kiss. It was blunt, that kiss. A little messy. She loved the way he was with her—raw and unchecked. Except he wasn't really unchecked. Even now, as carnal as he was, he held something back. She'd always assumed it had to do with him. With his time in the army or his perception of himself as a monster.

But a new thought occurred to her, especially after the events of the day, after the careful and cruel incision into her fears. What if he held back because of *her*? Because he didn't know if she could handle him.

There was a time she would have scoffed at the idea. Of course she could handle anything he did to her body, her mind. She craved it. But now, feeling stripped down and abraded, she wasn't so sure. And yet that didn't stop her from wanting him.

If she was going to break, she wanted him to be the one to break her.

"Fuck me," she whispered.

"What?" He pulled back to meet her eyes. It wasn't the language she usually used with him, and there was a question in his eyes. Did she really want this? Was she too upset to make decisions for herself?

It made her angry. And it made her sad. She shoved at his chest with her fists. "I said fuck me."

"Erin, baby. I'll make you feel good."

That was him, making her come, making her shudder and scream her way through climax. *Let me take care of you.* He was such a good man. But for tonight, she wanted him to be bad.

She shoved him again, her forearms against his body. "Not good, Blake. Hard. Do it hard."

His eyes flashed with something dangerous—

and seductive. "You don't want it like this."

"Don't tell me what I want. I want to feel…" She considered all the things she wanted to feel. Pain. Pleasure. The soul-deep uncertainty that she had somehow named love. In the end, it was simpler than that. "I just want to *feel.*"

He took a step back. "I love you."

She followed him, placing a hand on his chest, petting him, apologizing if she'd hurt him. "Then fuck me like you mean it. Do whatever you want with me."

The decision came faster than she was expecting. And it came in the form of his hand in her hair, pulling back, turning her face up to the sky. She gasped but let her body hang by his touch.

"You want me to be rough, is that it?" His words were soft against her cheek.

"Yes," she managed.

"You want to see what I'm really like when I don't hold back."

"*Yes.*"

"Because you still don't know me." His words sounded more sad than offended. "You still think there's going to be something sweet and loving. That I can just give you a spanking on the soft part of your ass, like this is a *game*, and I'll be able to stop there."

She shivered. "Show me then."

His hand tightened in her hair. "It's not a fucking game."

He bent his head and licked at her throat. Then he bit her, teeth scraping along her jaw as she cried out to the moon. Her hands fumbled for his shoulders, his arms, trying to hold on.

"No," he said coldly. "You don't get to hug me and cuddle me, not when you want me to *fuck* you. Not when you want me to show you the real me."

He dragged her by her hair in one hand, and her upper arm in the other, to a tree. Then he pushed her against it, face first. He positioned her arms around the tree as if she were a doll, making her hug the tree. He undid her jeans and yanked them down to her knees, using them like a rope, tying her still. And he shoved her shirt and bra up, exposing her skin to the air and the tree.

"Like that," he said, a hardness in his voice she didn't understand. "You stay just like that no matter what I do to you. And when I'm done, your breasts will be red and raw, and I won't even have touched them. Understand?"

She whimpered, aroused and nervous and somehow floating. It *was* freeing for him to speak to her this way, for him to hurt her like this. It was freeing not to know what would happen next.

What happened next was a blunt finger pressing inside her pussy from behind. She gasped, her mouth open against the tree.

"Wet," he murmured. "Are you always this wet? Do you walk around all day during class or work with your pussy slick as a waterfall? Or is that just for me, every fucking time?"

She shuddered. "For you," she said, her voice high and thin. "It's for you."

Then his fingers were at her mouth. "Taste yourself," he demanded.

Before she had a chance to respond, to even think about saying no, he pushed inside. She sucked on his fingers obediently, licking her juices off his coarse skin. When he was satisfied, he removed his hand. Then his heat was at her back, his cock nudging her entrance.

"You want me to scare you," he whispered. "That way you can walk away tomorrow for what happened today. Prove that I'm really like my father. That I'm a rich bastard willing to take what he wants, *who* he wants, and damn the consequences."

Dark realization washed over her. He thought she was doing this because she wanted out. He thought she was using his sexuality—his pain—

against him. "No," she cried.

"Yes," he gritted out, thrust inside her.

The fullness shocked her, and she lifted up on her toes, trying to escape. Her breasts shoved against the bark of the tree, making her whimper. There was no escape, only invasion, only pain. Only the knowledge that he was finally letting her in.

"Blake. *Blake.*"

"I shouldn't touch you when you're like this, when it's going to be the last fucking time, but I can't help it. You pushed me and pushed me, and now you're getting it. How does it feel, baby? How does the bark feel on your skin? How does my dick feel in your cunt?" As if to punctuate his words, he slipped his hand around and pinched her clit—hard. "This is what I want to do to you, all the fucking time. This is how it would be if I didn't hold back. Fucking you, using you, tearing you up."

He pulled back and thrust inside, and she couldn't deny that she was being fucked and used. It even felt like being torn, rent into two parts from the inside, his cock so deep and thick inside her.

"I never want this to end," she gasped.

"You will," he promised.

And then he sped up, moving quickly as he thrust, his cock pulling far out only to slam back inside, her breasts bouncing against the rough curve of the tree, her cries echoing around the clearing and over the city.

"Tell me what she said to you," he gritted out. "Tell me why you're hurting."

And it hurt more than the bark, more than his cock, to answer him. "She said I wasn't good enough for you. That I was trash. That I would always be trash."

"Fuck," he growled, sounding savage. Like he could rip her apart. "That's not fucking true."

"I know," she sobbed, but she didn't know, not really. And it was hard to talk with him still fucking her, not as fast as before, but still enough that each word rode on a breath, choppy and short. Because as hard as it was to talk like this, it was the only way she *could* talk. "But I thought… I didn't know… God, we're so different, Blake."

Another growl, this one wordless and animalistic. "That's where you're wrong. We're the same, you and me. I'll fucking make us the same."

It seemed impossible that it could work, that he could somehow fuck them into the same person. But that was how it felt, his cock impaling her, the incredible wet friction between their bodies fusing them together.

His other hand slapped her ass, the sound resounding in the stillness. "Moan," he said, guttural. "I want to hear you."

So she let herself moan—and also talk and babble and cry against that tree, hugging it and being hugged by Blake, even while he brutally fucked her. There were words and apologies and explanations. There were garbled sounds even she couldn't make out. And then there was only a steady litany. "I love you I love you I love you."

His hips jerked roughly as he came, and it was the feel of him coming, his hands gripping her hips, surely leaving bruises, a hot gush of seed deep inside, that made her come too. She rocked her hips, humping the tree, as her orgasm slammed into her.

He rode the last of the pulses with languid patience, letting her pulse and spasm around his cock, feeling his seed slide down on him. When she had finished and slumped against the tree, he gently pulled away. He righted his clothes, and then hers, and then placed a kiss on her nape.

"Thank you for telling me."

She smiled into the dark, her face half hidden by the tree. "Thank you for fucking me."

"It's bullshit, you know. The idea that we're

so different. That you're not good enough." He turned her around and leaned her back against the tree, letting her rest against it but looking her right in the eye. "When I look at you, I see everything I want to be."

She let her eyes fall shut as he kissed her forehead. "I love you."

"Love you too, baby." He ran a finger over the curve of her breast. "Are you sore?"

Her breasts would be tender for days. She loved it. "As awful as this day was, it might be worth it for the tree sex."

He laughed softly. "You know, there are a lot of trees on the property back home."

"We should probably draw a map. For surveying purposes."

"Mhmm. We wouldn't want to miss one."

CHAPTER SEVENTEEN

BLAKE

BLAKE TOOK IN the thin carpet of the apartment hallway, the faint smell of mold overlaid with something sweet—chocolate. With the dim overhead lights and all of the doors shut, it was grim. Hard to imagine a young Erin bounding home from school with a backpack slung over her shoulder and a cheeky grin on her face. This wasn't a building that inspired smiles.

But that's what Sofia was doing when she opened the door—smiling. She had a huge smile on her face as she embraced her daughter.

"Mama, I missed you so much."

Sofia turned to him, and he was shocked to see tears in her eyes. Then Sofia collected him in a hug. Somehow it happened exactly like that despite her being shorter and smaller—he found himself embraced and even squished by her. After a beat of surprise, he hugged her back. Erin looked at them with tears in her brown eyes—so like her mother's—and he knew this was how they both looked when they were happy.

His voice was surprisingly thick when he said, "It's good to see you, Mrs. Rodriguez."

In his life he'd been a son and a boyfriend and a fiancé. But he had never been hugged, only hugged, until Erin. And her mother. He supposed this is what family felt like.

"You don't know how much I worried about Erin," she said. "She is so strong, too strong. I worried she wouldn't let anyone in."

It felt like she was giving him her blessing, and it was a gift. He was grateful when she didn't make him respond, just nodded as if something had been decided there in that dingy hallway.

He picked up their bags and followed both women inside.

In the bright light of the kitchen, Sofia gasped. "Erin, what happened to your face?"

Guilt raced through him because across her jaw was a raw, red mark from the tree. Apparently his own scars couldn't shock Mrs. Rodriguez, but the evidence of their sex would need to be explained.

A pink blush covered Erin's cheeks. "We took a detour to a hiking spot Blake knew. I ended up face-first in a tree." She sent Blake a secret smile.

"Clumsy."

Sofia seemed to consider her daughter. After a moment, she relaxed. "I'll get some ointment. It doesn't look too deep, but just to be sure. Meanwhile both of you have a seat. And have some cookies."

He and Erin obediently sat at the small kitchen table where a plate of warm cookies sat waiting for them.

She grinned at him as she took one. "Busted."

He blinked. The sex? "Your mom didn't know."

Erin took a bite. "She knows."

"No way."

"I got my Trailblazer patch when I was eight. I've hiked all year round. I don't run into trees. But don't feel bad. She knew and she let you stay. That means you're in."

A warm, full feeling entered his chest. It didn't help that the cookie tasted like sugar and heaven. This felt a little like he'd thought home should feel. And family. And a childhood he'd never had. In some ways he'd grown up privileged, and for that he felt both shame and gratitude. But in other ways, he'd never known until now the quiet, powerful contentedness of belonging.

ERIN

ERIN LAY AWAKE, unable to sleep, even as Blake rumbled peacefully through a dream behind her. A few minutes later she gave up and carefully slipped out of his arms. She padded out of the bedroom to find her mother sitting on the sofa with a book open in her lap, eyes staring sightlessly in front of her.

She snapped her attention to Erin as she entered. "What's wrong? Do you need something to eat?"

Erin laughed softly. "Definitely not. You stuffed both of us full of enchiladas. And then the tres leches cake. I think I ate three slices of that cake."

Her mother couldn't hide her pleased look, almost smug. She enjoyed feeding people, and had especially liked the way Blake could pack it away. "I can give you the recipe."

"The enchiladas, yes. I don't think I should bake that cake, not when Blake and I can eat almost the entire thing in one sitting."

Her mother patted the cushion beside her. "Come sit then, if you're having trouble sleeping."

Erin sat down on the worn couch. She'd spent hours here, studying for a test or watching TV or reading quietly beside her mother. This couch was more her home than the city or the house ever had been. And so it gave her the strength to bring up the topic that had kept her awake.

"Mama, remember I told you that Blake is Senator Morris's son."

Her mother grew still. "Yes, I remember."

"And I know you used to work for them once."

"Yes." The word came softer now. It sounded almost afraid, and Erin didn't want to continue. She didn't want to be the one to hurt her mother, but she couldn't continue as if she didn't know.

"Blake's father told him that you two were... involved."

A long silence with only the distant, muffled sound of a slamming car door to fill it. "That's true," her mother finally said. "I was young... not as young as you. But much more foolish than you."

Erin frowned. "It's not foolish to fall for someone, even if they're not a good man. We can't control who we love. You taught me that."

"That's right, but you should know, Jeb—Mr. Morris—was a good man. He just made a mistake. There's a difference."

"A mistake? He let you get thrown out. He didn't defend you."

"I didn't mean that, sweetheart. I meant having an affair. He cheated on his wife. And even if he cared about me when he did it, that doesn't make it right."

Erin had a hard time sympathizing with the Ice Queen after their encounter, but she knew her mother was right. "I guess."

"And I knew he was married too. I shouldn't have gotten involved with him. I risked my job for that, and I lost it. I risked our family's income and being able to care for you." Her mother sighed, shaking her head. "Like I said, foolish."

Erin took her hand. She knew how strong her mother was—cleaning houses was intense physical labor. And yet her mother's hand felt small, almost frail. She squeezed. "I'm sorry for how it turned out, but I never would have wanted you to hold back, to *not* take a chance on love, just because you had me."

"Now you understand why I worried for you. That you saw me as a role model, holding myself tight, afraid to be hurt. I feared you would do the same."

In some ways Erin had done that. She'd blamed being busy with school and work for her lack of relationships. But she could have tried more, if she'd wanted to. She could have taken a chance on love, just like she'd told her mother. Even with Doug, she'd held herself back. It hadn't been until Blake that she'd been able to do that. Seeing him every week and then every day, learning the kind of man he was. Knowing that he would always protect her.

And finally letting go.

Chapter Eighteen

Blake

"MOVE," THE MAN shouted into his headset—telling the pilot to go.

Blake moved to jump out, but the man blocked him. The other man had fifty pounds on him, as well as more nights of sleep in the past 72 hours and more food and water. But Blake had the fucking determination, the certainty that he couldn't, wouldn't leave his teammate behind. His last one. The only man left. If it was anyone left on this rock, in this oven, it would be him.

A shot hit the chopper—impossible to know where. It rocked the whole machine, and Blake fell off balance. The doors were still open, but tilted up, and Blake was sliding back, falling. Every second took him farther from Ricardo, every second took him one more foot in the air.

"No," he roared, lunging for the doors. It would almost kill him to make the jump now, but he didn't care. This wasn't happening. This couldn't fucking *be happening.*

The guy caught him by the ankle just as he was almost out of the chopper.

He landed hard on the metal grate. The force of his fall swung the chopper far enough that he could see over the edge: the man sprawled on the ground, wounded. And he could see the other men, closing in now that the chopper was leaving range, surrounding him like a pack of wolves.

"No." This time it was only a quiet sound, stricken. Too soft to hear over the roar of the bird.

Ricardo's brother. Ricardo.

Something wasn't right. The bullet must have struck something vital, because the engine was sputtering now. They were still in the air but shifting sideways. At this height they'd crash. They'd burn.

And then they didn't have to wait that long. A flare of orange out of the corner of his eye was the only clue the chopper would explode in the split seconds before it did, before flames engulfed him, before the force of the blast threw him from the chopper, and then he was falling, falling out of the sky.

BLAKE

"BLAKE!"

He jerked awake, heart pumping, body

primed to fight an enemy that no longer existed. It took him a second to orient himself, to remember that he was no longer in the jungle in full combat gear, that he wasn't even in his house and his bed, but was instead in Erin's childhood room.

He panted while Erin stroked his back.

"Did I hurt you?" he asked.

She hesitated. She knew he wanted the truth, not just some false assurance he would have to doubt every time. "You caught me on the arm while I was trying to wake you up. It doesn't even hurt anymore, I'm just telling you so you won't worry."

He still worried, he couldn't help but worry. He loved her. It had been a kind of death sentence, finishing off the man he'd been so he could rise from the ashes. And now he was this man, one who worried with every breath he took, one who spent every waking second wanting to give her what she needed.

Only in his dreams did he lose himself in his old life. In his dreams and in the moments after them, when his body still shook with the need to fight, to fuck, to claim her in a primitive way. He'd held himself back from her before. Made himself wait. He'd stood at the window to his room until he felt enough like his regular self to touch her.

There wasn't a window to stand at here. There wasn't anywhere to go in the cramped room and he had no intention of leaving it. And besides, he'd learned over the course of this trip that he didn't need to hold back. He wasn't a thoughtful, kind, gentle lover when he was like this, but she didn't need him to be. Instead he was selfish and crude. He took what he needed from her body like a thirsty man would drink from a lake, with no thought to the lake's comfort or whether the lake needed the water more.

When would the nightmares stop?

He knew the answer now. They wouldn't stop, not ever, but somehow there was still hope. There was still this woman beside him, her body for solace, her heart to love.

Her eyes were wide—not with fear but acceptance. He pushed her back and shoved her nightgown up.

Bare.

She wasn't wearing any panties. His brain seemed to short out, and any semblance of reasoning fled. He shoved his pajama bottoms down and pressed his body between her legs, forcing her legs wide.

He stroked his cock once, twice, while she lay spread for him, waiting. He didn't say anything to her; he was beyond words. He dipped his fingers into her pussy and took the wetness there—not for her clit, but for his cock, fisting himself with her arousal.

Then he braced himself over her, fitted the head of his cock to her opening, and drove himself home.

She gasped and reached for him, but that wasn't what he wanted. Any other time he loved for her to touch him, loved for her to be free. But this was about using her—her body, her heart. This was about taking what was his. And so he grabbed her wrists together and held them over her head. He used his other hand to hold her hips steady as he fucked her hard enough to shake the bed.

He fucked her until his body was covered in a sheen of sweat, until his muscles were wound tight—until her pussy spasmed around him three separate times. Her body was limp beneath him, wrung out, and still he kept fucking her. This was what he was: an animal, a machine. A soldier. Something that could thrust and invade and fight for hours, and that was what he did.

"Can't," she whispered.

But he felt her tightening around him already, felt the gush of liquid heat his cock. He had no mercy in this moment. It was why he'd never touched her like this before. She'd wanted him—the real him, even at this time. And he knew that she could take it. So he gave it to her, hips pistoning, hand on her wrists, holding her on his cock, forcing her to come again.

It brought her to life, the orgasms, making her limp body buck and rock against him, shaking her breasts loose from the lacy fabric of her nightgown. Her brown nipples were stark against her pale skin, and he reached down to lick them. Only then, only sucking her firm, pebbled skin did his balls clamp down, did his come shoot deep inside her, did a groan rip from him, helpless with relief.

Even after he had come, he remained in her, thrusting lazily, enjoying the wet slide of her around his softening cock, using her to wring the final pulses of pleasure from his body.

"You okay?" he asked, his voice like gravel.

"Yeah," she answered, breathless and sleepy. "Don't move, okay? Stay."

He could do nothing but obey her—his woman, his salvation—and remain inside her as he drifted off to sleep, knowing he was too heavy but unable to stop the slide, shifting just enough that she'd be able to breathe.

"Forever," he promised.

In seconds her breathing evened out, and he knew she was asleep. He followed her down, still joined, her legs cradling him, her pussy cradling him, her breasts cradling him. And he took without remorse all she had to offer, all her comfort and softness and beauty. He covered her in both possession and protection, knowing he would never let her go.

EPILOGUE

BLAKE

Six months later

BLAKE EYED A tree in the distance. It was really the perfect tree. He couldn't imagine why he'd never realized it before. His vantage point was new. They'd set up the wedding arch in the very back of the property where a stream babbled in the distance. From here he could see the back of the house with the bright red hummingbird feeder and new gazebo. Erin had turned his house into a home, and he thought he might have always wanted that, longed for it, even when he could only pay her to dust the furniture.

He glanced at the woman beside him. His lover. And in a matter of minutes, his wife.

The pastor was taking his time.

Her eyes sparkled at him from underneath the veil as if she knew how impatient he was. He would have dragged her to the courthouse the day she said yes if he hadn't known she wanted a ceremony. So he'd nodded and smiled through the fittings and the tastings and the meetings with the designer. The end result, he had to admit, was fit for a princess—and he knew that it had all been worth it.

Well, it would be worth it if it could end soon.

He had sat through a long sermon about loyalty and love. He had spoken vows he'd written himself and listened to Erin's vows without choking up visibly in front of their small group of friends and family—an extreme achievement, he thought. He'd slipped a ring on her finger, a thin gold band to match the antique engagement ring she wore. And let her put a ring on his finger, pretending not to notice the way her hands shook.

And after that had begun the longest pronouncement of a union he'd ever heard. He forced himself to stay still. Forced himself not to send a silent message with his eyes to the pastor to finish already. With his scars and his dress uniform, it might come off more intimidating than he intended.

"You may now kiss the bride."

Thank fuck.

He lifted the thin veil and draped it behind

her, pulling her in close. His lips were an inch from hers, and still he hadn't kissed her. "How long until we kick everybody out?"

Her lips curved against his. "Hmm. Three hours?"

He groaned. "At least tell me you aren't wearing anything under that grown."

"I wouldn't dream of it."

"Good. Because there's a tree over there with our name on it. And the dress stays on."

Then he kissed her, his lips firm on hers, his tongue claiming, every movement a promise of what he'd do to her three hours later, of what he'd do for the rest of his life. To cherish and obey, to honor and protect, forever.

THE END

Thank you so much for reading FALLING FOR THE BEAST. I hope you loved Blake and Erin's emotional and erotic story! If you enjoyed this duet, you'll love OVERTURE, a new forbidden romance.

Forbidden fruit never tasted this sweet...

"Swoon-worthy, forbidden, and sexy, Liam North is my new obsession."

—New York Times bestselling author
Claire Contreras

The world knows Samantha Brooks as the violin prodigy. She guards her secret truth—the desire she harbors for her guardian.

Liam North got custody of her six years ago. She's all grown up now, but he still treats her like a child. No matter how much he wants her.

No matter how bad he aches for one taste.

"Overture is a beautiful composition of forbidden love and undeniable desire. Skye

has crafted a gripping, sensual, and intense story that left me breathless. Get ready to be hooked!"

—USA Today bestselling author Nikki Sloane

Turn the page for an excerpt from OVER-TURE…

EXCERPT FROM OVERTURE

EST, LIAM TOLD me.

He's right about a lot of things. Maybe he's right about this. I climb onto the cool pink sheets, hoping that a nap will suddenly make me content with this quiet little life.

Even though I know it won't.

Besides, I'm too wired to actually sleep. The white lace coverlet is both delicate and comfy. It's actually what I would have picked out for myself, except I didn't pick it out. I've been incapable of picking anything, of choosing anything, of deciding anything as part of some deep-seated fear that I'll be abandoned.

The coverlet, like everything else in my life, simply appeared.

And the person responsible for its appearance? Liam North.

I climb under the blanket and stare at the ceiling. My body feels overly warm, but it still feels good to be tucked into the blankets. The blankets *he* picked out for me.

It's really so wrong to think of him in a sexual way. He's my guardian, literally. Legally. And he has never done anything to make me think he sees *me* in a sexual way.

This is it. This is the answer.

I don't need to go skinny dipping in the lake down the hill. Thinking about Liam North in a sexual way is my fast car. My parachute out of a plane.

My eyes squeeze shut.

That's all it takes to see Liam's stern expression, those fathomless green eyes and the glint of dark blond whiskers that are always there by late afternoon. And then there's the way he touched me. My forehead, sure, but it's more than he's done before. That broad palm on my sensitive skin.

My thighs press together. They want something between them, and I give them a pillow. Even the way I masturbate is small and timid, never making a sound, barely moving at all, but I can't change it now. I can't moan or throw back my head even for the sake of rebellion.

But I can push my hips against the pillow, rocking my whole body as I imagine Liam doing more than touching my forehead. He would trail his hand down my cheek, my neck, my shoulder.

Repressed. I'm so repressed it's hard to imagine more than that.

I make myself do it, make myself trail my hand down between my breasts, where it's warm and velvety soft, where I imagine Liam would know exactly how to touch me.

You're so beautiful, he would say. *Your breasts are perfect.*

Because Imaginary Liam wouldn't care about big breasts. He would like them small and soft with pale nipples. That would be the absolute perfect pair of breasts for him.

And he would probably do something obscene and rude. Like lick them.

My hips press against the pillow, almost pushing it down to the mattress, rocking and rocking. There's not anything sexy or graceful about what I'm doing. It's pure instinct. Pure need.

The beginning of a climax wraps itself around me. Claws sink into my skin. There's almost certain death, and I'm fighting, fighting, fighting for it with the pillow clenched hard.

"Oh fuck."

The words come soft enough someone else might not hear them. They're more exhalation of breath, the consonants a faint break in the sound.

I have excellent hearing. Ridiculous, crazy good hearing that had me tuning instruments before I could ride a bike.

My eyes snap open, and there's Liam, standing there, frozen. Those green eyes locked on mine. His body clenched tight only three feet away from me. He doesn't come closer, but he doesn't leave.

Orgasm breaks me apart, and I cry out in surprise and denial and relief. "*Liam.*"

It goes on and on, the terrible pleasure of it. The wrenching embarrassment of coming while looking into the eyes of the man who raised me for the past six years.

Want to read more? OVERTURE is available on Amazon, iBooks, Barnes & Noble, Kobo, and other book retailers!

MORE BOOKS BY SKYE WARREN

Endgame trilogy & Masterpiece Duet

The Pawn

The Knight

The Castle

The King

The Queen

Trust Fund Duet

Survival of the Richest

The Evolution of Man

North Security series

Overture

Concerto

Underground series

Rough

Hard

Fierce

Wild

Dirty

Secret

Sweet

Deep

Stripped series

Tough Love

Love the Way You Lie

Better When It Hurts

Even Better

Pretty When You Cry

Caught for Christmas

Hold You Against Me

To the Ends of the Earth

Standalone Books

Wanderlust

On the Way Home

Beauty and the Beast

Anti Hero

Escort

About the Author

Skye Warren is the New York Times bestselling author of contemporary romance such as the Chicago Underground and Stripped series. Her books have been featured in Jezebel, Buzzfeed, USA Today Happily Ever After, Glamour, and Elle Magazine. She makes her home in Texas with her loving family, two sweet dogs, and one evil cat.

Sign up for Skye's newsletter:
www.skyewarren.com/newsletter

Like Skye Warren on Facebook:
facebook.com/skyewarren

Join Skye Warren's Dark Room reader group:
skyewarren.com/darkroom

Follow Skye Warren on Instagram:
instagram.com/skyewarrenbooks

Visit Skye's website for her current booklist:
www.skyewarren.com/books

COPYRIGHT

This is a work of fiction. Any resemblance to actual persons, living or dead, business establishments, events or locales is entirely coincidental. All rights reserved. Except for use in a review, the reproduction or use of this work in any part is forbidden without the express written permission of the author.